先进篇第十一 (共二十六章)

Remark about Confucius£§Students

11.1

子曰："先进于礼乐¹，野人也²；后进于礼乐，君子也³。如用之，则吾从先进。"

【中译文】

孔子说："先学习礼乐之后做官的人，是布衣子弟；先做官而后学习礼乐的人，是卿大夫的子弟。如果要选用人才，我将选用先学习礼乐的人。"

【注释】

1 "先进"句：指先在学习礼乐方面有所进益，先掌握了礼乐方面的知识。"后进"反之。

2 野人：这里指庶民，没有爵禄的平民。与世袭贵族相对。

3 君子：这里指有爵禄的贵族，世卿子弟。

【英译文】

The Master (Confucius) said, 'Only common people wait until they are advanced in ritual and music before taking office. A gentleman can afford to get up his ritual and music later on.' Even if I accepted this saying, I should still be on the side of those who learned ritual and music first.

11.2

子曰："从我于陈、蔡者¹，皆不及门也²。"

【中译文】

孔子说："曾经随从我在陈国、蔡国的弟子们，如今都不在我的门下了。"

【注释】

1 "从我"句：公元前489年（鲁哀公四年，当时孔子六十一岁），孔子周游列国，率领弟子们从陈国去蔡国。途中，楚国派人来聘请孔子，孔子将往楚国拜礼了。陈、蔡大夫怕与己不利，便派徒役在郊野围困孔子。孔子和弟子们断粮七天，许多人饿得不能行走。后由子贡去楚国告急，楚昭王派兵前来迎孔子，才获解救。当时随从孔子的弟子有子路、子贡、颜回等。公元前484年，孔子返回鲁国后，子路、子贡等先后离开，有的做了官，有的回老家，颜回也病死了。孔子时常思念那些在艰危中跟随他的弟子们。

2 不及门："门"，指学习、受教育的场所。"及"，在，到。不及门，指到不了、不在他的门下受教育。一说，是"不及仕进（卿大夫）之门"，"孔子弟子无仕陈蔡者"。

【英译文】

The Master (Confucius) said, My adherents in Chen and Cai States were

11.2

子曰："从我于陈、蔡者，皆不及门也。"

【中译文】

孔子说："当初跟从我在陈、蔡两国的学生，如今都不在我的门下了。"

【注释】

【英译文】

The Master (Confucius) said, My adherents in Chen and Cai States were

---

先进篇第十一 (六二十六章)

Remark about Confucius's Students

11.1

子曰："先进于礼乐，野人也；后进于礼乐，君子也。如用之，则吾从先进。"

【中译文】

孔子说："先学习礼乐而后做官的人，是原来未有爵禄的平民；先有了爵位而后学习礼乐的人，是卿大夫的子弟。如果要我选用人才，我主张选用先学习礼乐的人。"

【注释】

【英译文】

The Master (Confucius) said, 'Only common people wait until they are advanced in ritual and music before taking office. A gentleman can afford to get up his ritual and music later on. Even if I accepted this saying, I should still be on the side of those who learned ritual and music first.

【中译文】

孔子说："颜回啊，不是能帮助我的人，他对我所说的话，没有不心悦诚服的。"

【注释】

1 说：同"悦"。这里是说颜回对孔子的话从来不提出疑问或反驳。

【英译文】

The Master (Confucius) said, Yan Hui was not any help to me; he fully accepted everything I said.

11.5

子曰："孝哉闵子骞[1]！人不间于其父母昆弟之言[2]。"

【中译文】

孔子说："闵子骞，真孝顺啊！人们从他的父母兄弟称赞他孝的话中，找不出什么可挑剔的地方。"

【注释】

1 闵子骞：当时有名的孝子，被奉为尽孝的典范。他的孝行事迹被后人编入《二十四孝》。参阅《雍也篇第六》第九章。

2 间：挑剔，找毛病。昆：兄。

---

none of them in public service.

11.3

德行[1]："颜渊，闵了骞，冉伯牛，仲弓。言语[2]：宰我，子贡。政事[3]：冉有，季路。文学[4]：子游，子夏。"

【中译文】

德行好的有颜渊，闵子骞，冉伯牛，仲弓。擅长辞令的有宰我，子贡。善于行政事务的有冉有，季路。熟知诗书礼乐的有子游，子夏。

【注释】

1 德行：指能实行忠恕仁爱孝悌的道德。

2 言语：指长于应对辞令、办理外交。

3 政事：指管理国家，从事政务。

4 文学：指通晓西周文献典籍。

【英译文】

Yan Hui, Min Ziqian, Ran Boniu and Zhong Gong were famous for their virtues; Zai Wo and Zi Gong, for their eloquence; Ran You and Ji Lu, as administrators; Zi You and Zi Xia, for their literary acquirements.

11.4

子曰："回也非助我者也，于吾言无所不说[1]。"

论语意解

【英译文】

The Master (Confucius) said, Yan Hui was not of any help to me; he fully accepted everything I said.

【英译文】

Yan Hui, Min Ziqian, Ran Boniu and Zhong Gong were famous for their virtues; Zai Wo and Zi Gong, for their eloquence; Ran You and JH u. as administrators; Zi You and JZi Xia, for their literary acquirements.

... one of them in public service.

11.7

季康子问：“弟子孰为好学？”孔子对曰：“有颜回者好学，不幸短命死矣，今也则亡[1]。”

【中译文】

季康子问：“你的弟子中谁是爱好学习的呢？”孔子回答：“有一个叫颜回的，很好学，但不幸短命死了，如今还没有像他那样好学的了。”

【注释】

1 亡：同“无”。本章文字与《雍也篇第六》第三章略同，可参阅。

【英译文】

Ji Kangzi asked which of the disciples had a love of learning. The Master replied, There was Yan Hui. He was fond of learning, but unfortunately his allotted span was a short one, and he died. Now there is none.

11.8

颜渊死，颜路请子之车以为之椁[1]。子曰：“才、不才，亦各言其子也。鲤也死[2]。有棺而无椁。吾不徒行以为之椁。以吾从大夫之后[3]，不可徒行也。”

【英译文】

The Master (Confucius) said, Min Ziqian is indeed a very good son. No one can take exception to what his parents or brothers have said of him.

11.6

南容三复“白圭”[1]，孔子以其兄之子妻之[2]。

【中译文】

南容反复诵读关于“白圭”的诗句，孔子便把侄女嫁给了他。

【注释】

1 南容：即南宫适。参阅《公冶长篇第五》第二章注。三复：多次重复。“三”是虚数，指在一日之内多次诵读。白圭：指《诗经·大雅·抑》篇。其中有云：“白圭之玷，尚可磨也（白圭上的斑点污点，还可以磨掉）；斯言之玷，不可为也（言语中的错误，不能收回不能挽救了）。”意思 指：说话一定要小心谨慎。

2 妻：作动词用。以女嫁人。

【英译文】

Nan Rong in reciting The Book of poetry repeated the verse about the sceptre of white jade three times. In consequence of which the Master gave him his elder brother's daughter to marry.

11.7

季康子问：“弟子孰为好学？”孔子对曰：“有颜回者好学，不幸短命死矣，今也则亡。”

【中译文】

季康子问：“你的学生中谁是爱学习的呢？”孔子回答："有一个叫颜回的，很好学，但不幸短命死了，如今再也没有像他那样好学的了。”

【注释】

1亡：同“无”。本章文字与《雍也篇第六》第三章略同，可参阅。

【英译文】

Ji Kangzi asked which of the disciples had a love of learning. The Master replied, There was Yan Hui. He was fond of learning, but unfortunately his allotted span was a short one, and he died. Now there is none.

11.8

颜渊死，颜路请子之车以为之椁。子曰：“才不才，亦各言其子也。鲤也死，有棺而无椁。吾不徒行以为之椁。以吾从大夫之后，不可徒行也。”

【英译文】

The Master (Confucius) said, Min Ziqian is indeed a very good son. No one can take exception to what his parents or brothers have said of him.

11.6

南容三复“白圭”，孔子以其兄之子妻之。

【中译文】

南容反复诵读关于“白圭”的诗句，孔子便把哥哥的女儿嫁给了他。

【注释】

1南容：即南宫适。参阅《公冶长篇第五》第二章。2三复：多次重复。“三”是虚数。白圭：见《诗经·大雅·抑》篇。其中有云：“白圭之玷，尚可磨也（白玉上的现玷点污点，还可以磨掉）；斯言之玷，不可为也（言语中的错误，不能收回不能挽救了）。”意思是：说话一定要小心谨慎。2妻：作动词用，以女嫁人。

【英译文】

Nan Rong in reciting The Book of poetry repeated the verse about the sceptre of white jade three times. In consequence of which the Master gave him his elder brother's daughter to marry.

that he might use it to make the enclosure for the coffin. The Master said, Gifted or not gifted, you have spoken of your son and I will now speak of mine. When Li (the Master's son)died he had a coffin, but no enclosure. I did not go on foot in order that he might have an enclosure; for I rank next to the Great Officers and am not permitted to go on foot.

11.9

颜渊死。子曰："噫！天丧予[1]！ 天丧予"

【中译文】

　　颜渊死了。孔子说："咳呀！老天爷要我的命呀！老天爷要我的命呀！"

【注 释】

1 天丧予："丧"，亡，使……灭亡。孔子这句话的意思是，颜渊一死，他宣扬的儒道就无人继承，无人可　传了。

【英译文】

　　When Yan Hui died, the Master said, Alas, Heaven has bereft me, Heaven has bereft me!

11.10

颜渊死，子哭之恸[1]。从者曰："子恸矣！"曰："有恸乎？非夫人之为恸而谁为[2]？"

【中译文】

　　颜渊死了，颜路请求孔子卖了车给颜渊买个椁。孔子说："虽然颜渊有才、孔鲤无才，但对我们人说来都是自己的儿子啊。孔鲤死了，只有棺而没有椁。我不能卖掉车步行，来给他买椁。因为我过去当过大夫，是不可以步行的。"

【注 释】

1 颜路：姓颜，名无繇（yóu），字路，娶齐姜氏，生子颜回（颜渊）。颜路是孔子早年在故乡阙里教学时所收的第一批弟子，比孔子小六岁。生于公元前545年，卒年不详。椁（guǒ）：古代有地位的人，棺材有两层：内层直接装殓尸体，叫"棺"，有底；外面还套着一层套棺，叫"椁"，无底。合称"棺椁"。

2 鲤：孔鲤，孔子的儿子。孔子十九岁，娶宋国人亓官氏，生子伯鱼。生伯鱼时，鲁昭公以鲤鱼赐孔子，因此给儿子起名叫孔鲤。孔鲤五十岁死，时孔子七十岁。

3 从大夫之后：跟从在大夫们的后面。是自己曾是大夫（孔子任鲁国司寇，是主管治安与司法的行政长官）的　谦虚的表达方法。按礼大夫出门要坐车，否则为失礼 。

【英译文】

　　When Yan Hui died, his father Yan Lu begged for the Master's carriage,

论语意解

论语意解

11.9

颜渊死。子曰:"噫!天丧予!天丧予。"

【中译文】

颜渊死了。孔子哭喊:"哎呀!是天要夺我的命呀!是天要夺我的命呀!"

【注释】

1 天丧予:"丧","亡","使……亡"。孔子这句话的意思是,颜渊一死,他宣扬的儒道就无人继承,无人可传了。

【英译文】

When Yan Hui died, the Master said, Alas, Heaven has bereft me, Heaven has bereft me!

11.10

颜渊死,子哭之恸。从者曰:"子恸矣!"曰:"有恸乎?非夫人之为恸而谁为?"

【中译文】

颜渊死了,孔子哭得十分悲痛。跟随孔子的人说:"是太悲痛了吧。"孔子答道:"你对我们的悲痛很稀奇吗?不是自己的儿子吗,孔鲤死了,只有棺材而没有椁,未不能卖掉步行,来给他买椁。因为我这去当过大夫,是不可以步行的。"

【注释】

1 颜路:姓颜,名无繇(yóu),字路,子路,是齐美氏的子路之同门(颜渊)。颜路是孔子早年的名弟子,随其学时自已的一帮弟子,比孔子小六岁,生于公元前545年,卒不详。椁(guǒ):古代有地位的人,棺材有两层:内层直接装殓尸体,叫"棺",外面还套着一层套棺,叫"椁"。无椁,合称"棺椁"。

2 鲤:孔鲤,孔子的儿子,孔子十九岁,娶宋国人方氏,生子伯鱼,生旧姑射,鲁昭公以鲤赐题孔子,因此孔子起名叫孔鲤。孔鲤五十岁死,时孔子七十岁。

3 从大夫之后:跟从在大夫们后面,是自己曾是大夫(孔子任鲁国司寇,是主管治安与司法的长官)的谦虚的表达法。按礼大夫出门要坐车,否则违反失礼。

【英译文】

When Yan Hui died, his father Yan Lu begged for the Master's carriage, that he might use it to make the enclosure for the coffin. The Master said, Gifted or not gifted, you have spoken of your son and I will now speak of mine. When Li (the Master's son) died he had a coffin, but no enclosure. I did not go on foot in order that he might have an enclosure; for I rank next to the Great Officers and am not permitted to go on foot.

【中译文】

　　颜渊死了，孔子哭得很悲痛。跟随的人说："先生您太悲痛了！"孔子说："是太悲痛了吗？不为这样的人悲痛还为谁呢？"

【注释】

1　恸（tòng）：极度哀痛，悲伤。

2　"非夫人"句：即"非为夫人恸而为谁"的倒装。"夫"，指示代词，代指死者颜渊。"之"是虚词，在语法上只起到帮助倒装的作用。

【英译文】

When Yan Hui died, the Master wept for him. His followers said, Master, you are wailing without restraint! He said, Am I doing so? Well, if any man's death could justify abandoned wailing, it would surely be this man's!

11.11

　　颜渊死，门人欲厚葬之，子曰："不可。"门人厚葬之。子曰："回也视予犹父也，予不得视犹子也[1]。非我也，夫二三子也。"

【中译文】

　　颜渊死了，学生们想厚葬他。孔子说："不可以。"学生们仍然厚葬了颜渊。孔子说："颜回啊，看待我如同父亲，我却不能看待他如同儿子。不是我主张厚葬啊，是那些学生们呀。"

【注释】

1　"予不得"句：意谓我不能像对待亲生儿子那样按礼来安葬颜渊。孔子认为办理丧葬应"称家之有亡（无）"，当时颜渊家贫，办丧事铺张奢侈，与礼不合同时，按颜渊的身份与地位，也是不应该厚葬的。

【英译文】

When Yan Hui died, the disciples wanted to give him a grand burial. The Master said it would be wrong to do so; nevertheless they gave him a grand burial. The Master said, Yan Hui dealt with me as though I were his father. But I have failed to treat him as my son. The fault, however, is not mine. It is yours, my friends!

11.12

　　季路问事鬼神[1]。子曰："未能事人，焉能事鬼？"曰："敢问死。"曰："未知生，焉知死？"

【中译文】

　　子路问怎样事奉鬼神。孔子说："没能把人事奉好，哪能谈事奉鬼呢？"子路又说："我大胆地请问，死是怎么回事？"孔子说："还不知道人生的道理，怎能知道死呢？"

问："君孰与足？"

【注释】

1. "年不顺成(句)：意思是不能够对待来生孔子那样按礼来安葬颜渊。"非吾徒也"为此。"不家之礼也(矣)"。

2. 孔门的同学等经：为厚葬颜渊的事。与礼不合问题。我颜渊的身份与地位，也是不应该厚葬的。

【英译文】

When Yan Hui died, the disciples wanted to give him a grand burial. The Master said it would be wrong to do so; nevertheless they gave him a grand burial. The Master said, Yan Hui dealt with me as though I were his father. But I have failed to treat him as my son. The fault, however, is not mine. It is yours, my friends!

11.12

季路问事鬼神。子曰："未能事人，焉能事鬼？"曰："敢问死。"子曰："未知生，焉知死。"

【中译文】

子路问怎样奉事鬼神。孔子说："还不能对人奉祭，哪能谈祭奉鬼呢？"子路又说："冒昧问问，死是怎么回事？"孔子说："还不知道人生的道理，怎能知道死呢？"

论语译解

【中译文】

颜渊死了，孔子哭得很悲痛。跟随的人说："先生悲痛过分了！"孔子说："是太悲痛了吗？不为这样的人悲痛还为谁呢？"

【注释】

1. 恸(tòng)：极度悲痛，悲伤。

2. "非夫人"句：即"非为夫人恸而为谁"的倒装。"夫"，指示代词，代指死者颜渊。"之"，最后一问，倒装连上只是为到着加强反问的作用。

【英译文】

When Yan Hui died, the Master wept for him. His followers said, Master, you are wailing without restraint! He said, Am I doing so? Well, if any man's death could justify abandoned wailing, it would surely be this man's!

11.11

颜渊死，门人欲厚葬之。子曰："不可。"门人厚葬之。子曰："回也视予犹父也，予不得视犹子也。非我也，夫二三子也。"

【中译文】

颜渊死了，学生们想厚葬他，孔子说："不可以。"学生们仍然厚葬了颜渊，孔子说："颜回啊，看待我如同父亲，我却不能看待他如同儿子。不是我主张要厚葬

4 由：仲由，字子路。

5 "不得"句：指得不到善终，不能正常地因衰老而死。孔子虑子路过于刚勇，好斗取祸而危及生命。后来，子路果猝死于卫国的孔悝（kuī）之乱。"然"，语气词。

【英译文】

When attending the Master, Min Ziqian looked polite and upright; Zi Lu looked staunch; Ran You and Zi Gong looked genial and affable. The Master was plesed. But of Zi Lu the Master said, "I'm afraid he will not die in his bed."

11.14

鲁人为长府[1]。闵子骞曰："仍旧贯，如之何？何必改作？"子曰："夫人不言[2]，言必有中[3]。"

【中译文】

鲁国的执政者要改建国库长府。闵子骞说："仍旧沿袭老样子，怎么不行呢？何必改建呢？"孔子说："这个人不说则已，一说就一语中的。"

【注释】

1 鲁人：指鲁国的当权者季氏。为：制造。在这里是改建、翻修的意思。长府：鲁国国库名。一说宫室名。

2 夫人：这个人。指闵子骞。

论语意解

【注释】

1 季路：即子路。因仕于季氏，又称季路。参阅《为政篇第二》第十七章注。

【英译文】

Zi Lu asked how to serve ghosts and spirits. The Master said, Till you have learnt to serve men, how can you serve ghosts? Zi Lu then ventured upon a question about the dead. The Master said, Till you know about the living, how are you to know about the dead?

11.13

闵子侍侧[1]，誾誾如也[2]；子路，行行如也[3]；冉有、子贡，侃侃如也。子乐。"若由也[4]，不得其死然[5]。"

【中译文】

闵子侍立在孔子身边，表现出正直而恭顺的样子；子路，很刚强的样子；冉有、子贡，愉快而理直气壮的样子。孔子很高兴。但又担心说："像仲由这样过于勇猛刚强，恐怕不得好死呀。"

【注释】

1 闵子：即闵子骞。后人敬称"子"。

2 誾誾（yín）：和悦而能中正直言。

3 行行（hàng）：形容性格刚强勇猛。

论语意释

【英译文】

Zi Lu asked how to serve ghosts and spirits. The Master said, 'Till you have learnt to serve men, how can you serve ghosts?' Zi Lu then ventured upon a question about the dead. The Master said, 'Till you know about the living, how are you to know about the dead?'

11.13

【英译文】

When attending the Master, Min Ziqian looked polite and upright; Zi Lu looked staunch; Ran You and Zi Gong looked genial and affable. The Master was pleased. 'But if Zi,' the Master said, 'I'm afraid he will not die in his bed.'

11.14

【英译文】

The Master said, "Why is Zhong You playing the Se (a large horizontal musical instrument) at my doorway?" Thereupon the disciples showed little respect for Zhong You, but the Master explained, "What I meant was that Zhong You has really come to the guest house, but he has not yet entered the room."

11.16

子贡问："师与商也孰贤¹？"子曰："师也过，商也不及。"曰："然则师愈与²？"子曰："过犹不及³。"

【中译文】

子贡问："子张和子夏谁更贤良？"孔子说："师过了，商不够。"子贡说："那么是师比较好一些吗？"孔子说："做过了和做得不够，是同样不完美的。"

【注释】

1 师：即子张。才高意旷，做事常有过分之处。参阅《为政篇第二》第十八章注。商：即子夏。拘谨保守，做事常有不及之处。参阅《学而篇第一》第七章注。孰：谁。
2 愈：胜过、更好些，强一些。与：同"欤"。语气助词，表疑问。
3 犹：似，如，如同。

3 中(zhòng)：这里指说的话能正中要害，说到点子上。

【英译文】

When the men of Lu state were dealing with the question of the Long Treasury, MinZiqian said, What about restoring it on the old lines? I see no necessity for rebuilding it on a new plan. The Master said, That man is no talker, but when he does say anything, it is certain to be the point.

11.15

子曰："由之瑟奚为于丘之门¹！"门人不敬子路。子曰："由也升堂矣，未入于室也²。"

【中译文】

孔子说："仲由够得上在我这里弹瑟吗？"学生们因此不尊敬子路。孔子说："仲由啊，在学习上已经达到'升堂'的程度了，但是还没做到'入室'"。

【注释】

1 "由之瑟"句："瑟"，古代一种拨弦乐，二十五弦(一说五十弦)。"为"，做，弹瑟。"丘之门"，我(孔丘)这里。据《说苑·修文篇》，孔子对子路弹瑟表示不满，是因为子路性情刚猛，中和不足，故弹出的音调过于激励，"有杀伐之声"。
2 升堂、入室："堂"，正厅。"室"，内室。从入门，到升堂，再到入堂。孔子用此来比喻在学习上由浅入深的三个阶段：从入门初步掌握；到高明一些，达到一定水平；再到精微深奥的高妙境地。

论语意解

11.16

子贡问："师与商也孰贤？"子曰："师也过，商也不及。"曰："然则师愈与？"子曰："过犹不及。"

【中译文】

子贡问：“子张和子夏谁更贤良？”孔子说："师也过，商也不及。"子贡说："那么是师比较好一些吗？"孔子说："超过了和做得不够，是同样不完美的。"

【注释】

1. 师：即子张，办事常过火，概事常常有过分之处。参阅《先进篇第二》第十八章注。商：即子夏，拘谨怕事，碰事常常有不及之处。参阅《学而篇第一》第七章。

2. 愈：胜过，更好些，强一些。

3. 与：助词。

【英译文】

The Master said, "Why is Zhong You playing the Se (a large horizontal musical instrument) at my doorway?" Thereupon the disciples showed little respect for Zhong You, but the Master explained, "What I meant was that Zhong You has really come to the guest house, but he has not yet entered the room."

11.15

子曰："由之瑟奚为于丘之门？"门人不敬子路。子曰："由也升堂矣，未入于室也。"

【中译文】

孔子说："仲由弹瑟上在我这里弹些啥？"学生们因此不尊敬子路。孔子说："仲由啊，在学习上已经走到'升堂'的程度了，也是还没到'入室'。"

【注释】

1. "由之瑟"句："瑟"，古代一种拨弦乐器，一般二十五弦。（一说五十弦）。"之"，的。"奚"，疑问句。"为乎丘之门"，我（孔子）这里。据《说苑·修文篇》，孔子对子路弹瑟声表示不满，是因为子路性情刚猛，中和不足。故弹出的声音则凛厉，"杀伐之声"。

2. 孔之堂，入室："堂"，正厅。"室"，内室。从人家的门入到堂，再到入室，孔子用此来比喻治学由外人深的三个阶段，从入门初见基础，到有一定水平，再到精微深奥的高妙境地。

11.15 【英译文】

When the men of Lu state were dealing with the question of the Long Treasury, MinZiqian said, What about restoring it on the old lines? I see no necessity for rebuilding it on a new plan. The Master said, That man is no talker, but when he does say anything, it is certain to be the point.

数来征收，这就大大增加了赋税收入。冉求为季氏家臣，曾参与其事。孔子主张"敛从　其薄"，是反对　季氏、冉求这种过分剥削人民的做法的。

【英译文】

The head of the Ji Family was richer than Duke Zhou, yet Ran Qiu, by accumulating taxes for Ji, increased his wealth. Therefore, the Master declared, "He is no disciple of mine! Disciples, you have my permission to attack him with your drums rolling."

11.18

柴也愚[1]，参也鲁[2]，师也辟[3]，由也喭[4]。

【中译文】

高柴愚笨，曾参迟钝，颛孙师偏激，仲由莽撞。

【注释】

1 柴：姓高，名柴，字子羔。齐国人，身材很矮，为人笃孝。孔子的弟子。比孔子小三十岁，生于公元前521年，卒年不详。高柴老实，忠厚，正直，但明智变通不足，故孔子说他"愚"。

2 参也鲁："参"，曾参。曾参诚恳，信实，学习扎实深入，但反应有些迟钝，不够聪敏，故孔子说他"鲁"

3 师也辟："师"，颛孙师。"辟"，通"僻"，邪僻，偏激。颛孙师志向高，好夸张，习于容仪，但

论语意解

【英译文】

Zi Gong asked, "Who is the better man, Shi or Shang?" The Master said, "Shi often goes too far and Shang does not go far enough."

Zi Gong said, "In that case, Shi must be the better?" The Master said, "To go too far is as bad as not going far enough."

11.17

季氏富于周公[1]，而求也为之聚敛而附益之[2]。子曰："非吾徒也，小子鸣鼓而攻之可也。"

【中译文】

季氏比周朝的公卿还富，而冉求还要为季氏聚敛，进而更增加他的财富。孔子说："冉求不算是我的学生了，你们可以大张旗鼓去攻击他。"

【注释】

1 周公：周天子左右的公卿。如当时有周公黑肩、周公阅等人。鲁国之君，本是周公旦的后代，故用此比喻。

2 "而求也"句："求"，冉求。"也"，助词，用于句中，表示停顿，以引起下文。"之"，代指季氏。"聚敛（liǎn）"，聚积，收集，搜刮钱财。"而附益之"，而使季氏更增加了财富。鲁国本按"丘"(古代田地、区域的划分单位，四"邑"为一"丘")征收军　赋。公元前483年(鲁哀公十二年)，季康子改为按每一户的田亩

论语译注

11.17

季氏富于周公¹，而求也为之聚敛而附益之²。子曰："非吾徒也，小子鸣鼓而攻之可也。"

【中文译文】
季氏比周朝的公卿还要富，而冉求还是替季氏聚敛，进而增加他的财富。孔子说："冉求不再是我的学生了，你们可以大张旗鼓地去攻击他。"

【注释】
1. 周公：周天子左右的公卿，地位世有周公常居。周公阁等人。曾国之祖，本是周公旦的后代，故用此比喻。
2. 而求也："而"，犹"尔"，"汝来"。"也"，助词，用于句中，表停顿。以引而下文。"之"，代指季氏。"聚敛"（liǎn）："敛"，收集。魏起钱粮。"而附益之"，而使季氏更增加了财产富。曾国本接照列国分封单位，四"邑"为一"丘"，征收军赋。公元前483年（鲁哀公十二年），季康子改丘税为每一户的田亩征税，增加了赋税收入。再来为其长家宰，是帮凶，曾参与其事。孔子主张"薄赋敛"，是重农，反对"甲求及非只分剥削人民的做法而已"。

【英译文】
The head of the Ji Family was richer than Duke Zhou, yet Ran Qiu by accumulating taxes for it, increased his wealth. Therefore, the Master declared, "He is no disciple of mine! Disciples, you have my permission to attack him with your drums rolling."

11.18

柴也愚¹，参也鲁²，师也辟³，由也喭⁴。

【中文译文】
高柴愚笨，曾参迟钝，颛孙师偏激，仲由粗俗。

【注释】
1. 柴：高柴。名柴，字子羔，卫国人，身材短矮。孔子的弟子，比孔子小三十岁。生于公元前521年，卒年不详。"高柴足短，忠厚正直。心明智愚通不不"，故孔子说他"愚"。
2. 参也鲁："参"，曾参。曾参愚笨，不够聪敏，故孔子说他"鲁"。
3. 师也辟："师"，颛孙师。"辟"，通"僻"，邪癖。偏激。颛孙通志向高，好夸张，好方容貌。由：

【英译文】
Zi Gong asked, "Who is the better man, Shi or Shang?" The Master said, "Shi often goes too far and Shang does not go far enough." Zi Gong said, "In that case, Shi must be the better?" The Master said, "To go too far is as bad as not going far enough."

诚实不足，故孔子说他"辟"。

4 由也喭："由"，仲由。"喭（yàn）"，粗鲁，莽撞。仲由勇猛刚烈，但失于粗俗而文雅不足，故孔子说他"喭"。

【英译文】

(The Master (Confucius) said that) Gao Chai was stupid, Zeng Shen was dull, Chuansun Shi was extreme, Zhong You was rash.

11.19

子曰："回也其庶乎[1]，屡空[2]。赐不受命，而货殖焉[3]，亿则屡中[4]。"

【中译文】

孔子说："颜回嘛，差不多了吧，可是常常穷困。端木赐不接受命运安排，去做买卖，预测市场行情却常常能中。"

【注释】

1 庶：庶几，差不多。含有称赞之意。这里指颜回学问、道德都好。

2 空：指贫乏，困穷，穷得没办法。孔子曾说颜回："一箪食，一瓢饮，在陋巷，人不堪其忧，回也不改其乐。"（见《雍也篇第六》第十一章。）

3 货殖：做买卖，经商。

4 亿：同"臆"。估计，猜测。

【英译文】

The Master (Confucius) said, Yan Hui comes very near to it. He is often empty. Zi Gong was discontented with his lot and has taken steps to enrich himself. In his calculations he often hits the mark.

11.20

子张问善人之道[1]。子曰："不践迹，亦不入于室[2]。"

【中译文】

子张请问做善人的道理。孔子说："如果不跟着脚步走，怎么进入室内？"

【注释】

1 善人：孔子认为："善人"只是"质美（本质好）""欲仁"，所谓凭良心为善。然而，这是不够的。如果"善人"不循着前人（足可效法的先王圣贤）的脚步走，不通过学习去锻炼修养自己，也就达不到"入室"的高标准。

2 入于室：参见本篇第十五章注。

【英译文】

Zi Zhang asked about the Way of the good people. The Master said, He who does not tread in the tracks cannot expect to find his way into the Inner

【英译文】

The Master (Confucius) said, Yan Hui comes very near to it. He is often empty. Zi Gong was discontented with his lot and has taken steps to enrich himself. In his calculations he often hits the mark.

11.20

子张问善人之道。子曰："不践迹，亦不入于室。"

【中译文】

子张询问做善人的道理。孔子说："如果不沿着前辈的足迹，怎么进入室内？"

【注释】

1.善人：孔子认为，"善人"只是"尽美"（本原的）"，故仁，"即谓其见心为善，然而，这是本能的。如果"善人"不随着前人（乃可效法的先王圣贤）的脚印走，不通过学习去提炼修养自己，也很法不到"入室"的高标准。

2.入于室：参见本篇第十五章注。

【英译文】

Zi Zhang asked about the Way of the good people. The Master said, He who does not tread in the tracks cannot expect to find his way into the Inner

【英译文】

(The Master (Confucius) said that) Gao Chai was stupid, Zeng Shen was dull, Chuansun Shi was extreme, Zhong You was rash.

11.19

子曰："回也其庶乎，屡空。赐不受命，而货殖焉，亿则屡中。"

【中译文】

孔子说："颜回嘛，差不多了吧，可是常常贫困。赐不甘受命运安排，去做买卖，预测市场行情却常常能中。"

【注释】

1.庶：庶几，差不多。含有极赞之意。这里指赞回同学问、道德福近。

2.空：指贫乏，困穷。3.货殖：经商。孔子曾说颜回："一箪食，一瓢饮，在陋巷，人不堪其忧，回也不改其乐。"（见《雍也篇第六》第十一章。）

3.货殖：做买卖，经商。

4.由也喭："由"，仲由。"喭(yàn)"，粗俗。仲由勇猛过人，但失于粗俗而文雅不足，故孔子说他"喭"。

子曰'闻斯行之'。赤也惑[3]，敢问。"子曰：
"求也退，故进之；由也兼人[4]，故退之。"

【中译文】

子路问："是不是听到了就马上实行呢？"孔子说：
"有父兄在，怎么能不请示父兄就马上行动呢？"冉有
问："是否听到了就马上实行？"孔子说："听到了就
马上实行。"公西华问孔子说："仲由问'听到了就马
上实行吗'，您说'有父兄在'；冉求问'听到了就马
上实行吗'，您却说'听到了就马上实行'。这使我迷
惑不解，所以大胆地问个明白。"孔子说："冉求做事
畏缩不前，所以要鼓励他大胆前进一步；仲由一个人
能顶两个人，所以要约束他慎重一些。"

【注释】

1 斯：代词。这里代指道理，义理，应该做的事。
诸："之乎"二字合音。
2 求：即冉有。名求，字子有，也称冉有。
3 赤：即公西华。名赤，字子华，也称公西华。
4 兼人：指刚勇，敢作敢为，一个人能顶两个人。

【英译文】

Zi Lu asked, "Shall I put what I have heard into practice at once?" The Master said, "How can you do so while your father and elder brother are still alive?" Ran You asked the same question, however, the Master said, "Put it into practice immediately." Gongxi Hua then spoke up, "The replies you have

Room.

11.21

子曰："论笃是与[1]，君子者乎？色庄者乎[2]？"

【中译文】

孔子说："人们赞许言论诚恳笃实的人，问题真的
是君子呢？还是伪装出来的像君子一样庄重呢？"

【注释】

1 论笃是与：等于"与论笃"。"论笃"，言论诚恳
笃实的人。"与"，赞许。"是"无实义，起帮助"论笃"
这一宾语提前的语法作用。
2 色庄：神色庄重。这里指做出一副庄重的样子。

【英译文】

The Master said, That a man's conversation is sound one may grant. But whether he is indeed a true gentleman or easy merely one who adopts outwakl airs of solemnity, it is not so to say.

11.22

子路问："闻斯行诸[1]？"子曰："有父兄在，
如之何其闻斯行之？"冉有问："闻斯行诸？"子
曰："闻斯行之。"公西华曰："由也问'闻
斯行诸'，子曰'有父兄在'；求也问'闻斯行诸'[2]，

11.21

【英译文】

The Master said, That a man's conversation is sound one may grant. But whether he is indeed a true gentleman or easy merely one who adopts outward airs of solemnity, it is not so to say.

11.22

【英译文】

Zi Lu asked, "Shall I put what I have heard into practice at once?" The Master said, "How can you do so while your father and elder brother are still alive?" Ran You asked the same question, however, the Master said, "Put it into practice immediately." Gongxi Hua then spoke up, "The replies you have...

大臣者，以道事君，不可则止。今由与求也，可谓具臣矣[4]。"曰："然则从之者与？"子曰："弑父与君，亦不从也。"

【中译文】

季子然问："仲由、冉求能说是大臣吗？"孔子说："我以为您是问别的，原来是问仲由和冉求啊。所谓大臣，是能够用正道事奉君主的，如果不能这样，就宁可辞官不干。现在仲由和冉求，只可以说是具备做臣子的才能。"季子然说："那么他们做什么事都跟从季氏吗？"孔子说："如果杀父亲、杀君主那种事，也是不会听从的。"

【注释】

1 季子然：姓季孙，名平子，字子然，乃季孙意如之子。鲁国季氏的同族人。因为季氏任用子路、冉有为臣，所以，季子然向孔子提出了这一问题。
2 子：先生。尊称对方。为异之问：问的别的人。"异"，不同的，其他的。
3 曾：乃，原来是。
4 具臣：有做官的才能。"具"，才具，才能。

【英译文】

Ji Ziran asked whether Zhong You and. Ran Qiu could be called great ministers. The Master said, I thought you were going to ask some really inter-just given puzzled me and I beg for an explanation." The Master said, "Ran is apt to hang back, so I press him on; Zi Lu is bold and careless, so I hold him back."

11.23

子畏于匡[1]，颜渊后。子曰："吾以女为死矣。"曰："子在，回何敢死！"

【中译文】

孔子在匡地受到围困，颜渊最后才到。孔子惊喜地说："我以为你死了呢。"颜渊说："老师您还在，我怎么敢死呢？"

【注释】

1 畏：畏惧，有戒心。指孔子在匡地被人误以为是阳虎而受到围困。

【英译文】

When the Master was trapped in the place of Kuang, Yan Hui fell behind. The Master said, I thought you were dead. Yan Hui said, While you are alive how should I dare to die?

11.24

季子然问[1]："仲由、冉求可谓大臣与？"子曰："吾以子为异之问[2]，仲由与求之问[3]。所谓

first given me and I beg for an explanation." The Master said, "Ran is apt to hang back, so I press him on; Zi Lu is bold and careless, so I hold him back."

11.23

子畏于匡，颜渊后。子曰："吾以女为死矣。"曰："子在，回何敢死！"

【中译文】

孔子在匡地受到围困，颜渊最后才到。孔子说："我以为你已经死了。"颜渊说："老师您还活着，我怎么敢死呢？"

【注释】

1.畏：被围困。匡地在今河南省长垣县境内，孔子曾在此地被人围困。

【英译文】

When the Master was trapped in the place of Kuang, Yan Hui fell behind. The Master said, I thought you were dead. Yan Hui said, While you are alive how should I dare to die?

11.24

季子然问："仲由、冉求可谓大臣与？"子曰："吾以子为异之问，曾由与求之问。所谓……

又问："闻斯行诸，不可以为也。"今由与求也，可谓具臣矣。"曰："然则从之者与？"子曰："弑父与君，亦不从也。"

【中译文】

季子然问："仲由、冉求可以算是大臣吗？"孔子说："我以为你要问别的事，原来是问由和求啊。所谓大臣，是能够用正道事奉君主的，如果不能这样，就宁可辞官不干。现在仲由和冉求，只可以说是备位充数的臣属罢了。"季子然又问："那么他们肯听从君主吗？"孔子说："杀父亲杀君主的事，他们也是不会听从的。"

【注释】

1.季子然：鲁国季孙氏的同族人。因为孔子的弟子仲由、冉求都在季氏……

2.异：特别……

3.曾：乃，竟……

4.具臣：备位充数的臣属。

【英译文】

Ji Ziran asked whether Zhong You and Ran Qiu could be called great ministers. The Master said, I thought you were going to ask some really interesting question; and it is after all only a question about Zhong You and Ran Qiu! What I call a great minister is one who will only serve his prince while he can do so without infringement of the Way, and as soon as this is impossible, resigns. But in the present case, so far as concerns Zhong You and Ran Qiu, I should merely call them stop-gap ministers. Ji Ziran said, So you think they would merely do what they were told? The Master said, If called upon to slay their father or their prince, even they would refuse.

11.25

子路使子羔为费宰¹。子曰："贼夫人之子²。"子路曰："有民人焉，有社稷焉³，何必读书然后为学？"子曰："是故恶夫佞者⁴。"

【中译文】

　　子路让子羔去费地做长官。孔子说："这是害了人家的弟子。"子路说："那地方有百姓，有土地庄稼，何必非读书才算是学习呢？"孔子说："所以我讨厌狡辩的人。"

【注释】

1 子羔：高柴，字子羔。孔子弟子。比孔子小三十岁。
2 贼：害，毁坏，坑害。孔子认为子羔年轻，学业未成，让他从政，无异于害他。
3 社稷："社"，土地神。"稷(jì)"，谷神。古代说"社稷"，指祭祀土地神和谷神。后来又把"社稷"作为国家政权的象征。

4 恶(wù)：讨厌。佞(nìng)：巧言，谄媚。

【英译文】

　　Zi Lu got Zi Gao made the governor of Fei county. The Master said, You are doing an ill turn to another man's son. Zi Lu said, What he will take charge of at Pi will be the peasants and the Holy Ground and Millet. Surely 'learning consists in other things besides reading books'. The Master said, It is remarks of that kind that make me hate glib people.

11.26

　　子路、曾皙、冉有、公西华侍坐¹。

　　子曰："以吾一日长乎尔，毋吾以也²。居则曰³：'不吾知也！'如或知尔，则何以哉？"

　　子路率尔而对曰⁴："千乘之国⁵，摄乎大国之间⁶，加之以师旅⁷，因之以饥馑⁸，由也为之，比及三年⁹，可使有勇，且知方也¹⁰。"

　　夫子哂之¹¹。

　　"求！尔何如？"

　　对曰："方六七十，如五六十，求也为之，比及三年，可使足民。如其礼乐，以俟君子¹²。"

　　"赤¹³，尔何如？"

　　对曰："非曰能之，愿学焉。宗庙之事，如会同¹⁴，端章甫¹⁵，愿为小相焉¹⁶。"

论语意解

"点，尔何如？"

鼓瑟希[17]，铿尔[18]，舍瑟而作[19]，对曰："异乎三子者之撰[20]。"

子曰："何伤乎[21]？亦各言其志也。"

曰："莫春者[22]，春服既成[23]，冠者五六人[24]，童子六七人，浴乎沂[25]，风乎舞雩[26]，咏而归。"

夫子喟然叹曰："吾与点也！"

三子者出，曾皙后。曾皙曰："夫三子者之言何如？"

子曰："亦各言其志也已矣。"曰："夫子何哂由也？"

曰："为国以礼，其言不让。是故哂之。"

"唯求则非邦也与[27]？"

"安见方六七十如五六十而非邦也者？"

"唯赤则非邦也与？"

"宗庙会同，非诸侯而何，赤也为之小，孰能为之大？"

【中译文】

子路、曾皙、冉有、公西华，陪同孔子坐着。孔子说："我比你们年长一些，但不要因此有所拘束。你们平时常说：'人家不了解我啊！'假如有人想要了解你们，那么你们打算怎样做呢？"子路直爽回答说："拥有一千辆兵车的国家，夹在大国之间，受别国军队的侵犯，又遇上严重饥荒，让我治理，只要三年，就可以使人民勇敢，而且知道崇尚礼义。"孔子微笑了一下。又问："冉求，你如何呢？"冉求回答说："纵横六七十里，或者五六十里的小国，让我去治理，只要三年，就可以使人民富足。至于礼乐教化方面，那要等待君子去实行了。"孔子又问："公西赤，你如何呢？"公西赤回答说："不敢说我能够做到些什么，但我很愿意学习啊。在宗庙祭祀的事务上，或者与别的国家的盟会中，我穿上礼服，戴上礼帽，愿意做一个小小的司仪。"孔子又问："曾点，你如何呢？"曾点正在弹琴，铿的一声停了，放下琴，站起身来。回答说："我的志向不同于他们三位。"孔子说："那又有什么关系呢？也就是各人谈谈自己的志向啊！"曾点说："暮春时节，春天的夹服做好了，和五六个青年人，六七个少年，去沂河洗洗澡，到舞雩台上吹吹风，唱着歌一路走回来。"孔子长叹了一声，说："我是赞成曾点的。"三人出去了，曾皙最后走。曾皙问孔子说："他们三位说的话怎样呢？"孔子说："也就是各人谈谈自己的志向罢了。"曾皙说："夫子为何笑仲由呢？孔子说："治理国家要讲礼让，他说话却不谦让，所以我笑了。"曾皙又问："难道冉求所讲的不是邦国之事吗？"孔子说："哪里见得纵横六七十里或者五六十里的地方就不是国家呢？"

曾晳又问："难道公西赤所讲的不是邦国之事吗？"孔子说："有宗庙、有同别国的盟会，那不是诸侯国又是什么呢？如果公西赤只能做一个小司仪，谁还能做大的呢？"

【注释】

1 曾晳(xī)：姓曾，名点，字子晳。曾参的父亲。南武城人。也是孔子的弟子。
2 毋吾以：不要因我而受拘束，而停止说话，不肯发言。"毋"，不，不要。"以"，同"已"。停止。
3 居：平时，平素。
4 率尔：轻率地，急忙地。
5 千乘之国："乘(shèng)"，兵车。古代常以兵车数作为国家大小的标志。古代是按土地多少出兵车的，出一千辆兵车就是拥有纵横一百里面积的诸侯国。
6 摄：夹在其中，受局促，受逼迫，受管束。
7 师旅：古代军队组织，五人为伍，五伍为两，四两为卒(100人)，五卒为旅(500人)，五旅为师(2500人)，五师为军。"加之以师旅"，犹言发生战争，受别国军队的侵犯。
8 饥馑(jǐn)：荒年，灾荒，凶年。《尔雅·释天》："谷不熟为饥，蔬不熟为馑。"
9 比及：等到，到了。
10 知方：指懂得道义，遵守礼义。
11 哂(shěn)：微笑，讥笑。

12 俟(sì)：等待。
13 赤：即公西华。参阅《公冶长第五》第八章注。
14 会同：诸侯会盟。两诸侯相见，叫"会"；许多诸侯一起相见，叫"同"。
15 端章甫："端"，也写作"褍"，周代的一种礼服，也叫"玄端"。"章甫"，一种礼帽。这里泛指穿着礼服。
16 相：在祭祀、会同时，行赞礼的人员。也叫傧相。有不同的职位等级，故文中有"小相""大相"之说。
17 希：通"稀"。稀疏(节奏速度放慢)。
18 铿(kēng)尔：铿的一声。形容乐声有节奏而响亮。一说，曲终拨动瑟弦的馀音。
19 作：站起身来。
20 三子：三位。"子"是对同学的尊称。撰：同"譔"陈述的事，说的话。
21 伤：妨害，妨碍。
22 莫：同"暮"。
23 春服：指春天穿的夹衣(里表两层)。
24 冠者：成年人。古代男子二十岁举行冠礼，束发加冠，表示已经成年。
25 沂(yí)：水名。发源于山东省邹城市东北，经曲阜市南及江苏省北部，流入黄海。传说当时该处有温泉。

论语意解

26 风：作动词用，吹风，乘凉。舞雩："雩（yú）"，古代求雨的祭坛。因人们乞雨必舞，故称"舞雩"。这里指鲁国祭天求雨的台子，在今曲阜市南，有坛有树。北魏郦道元《水经注》称："沂水北对稷门，一名高门，一名雩门。南隔水有雩坛，坛高三丈，即曾点所欲风处也。"

27 唯：语首助词，无实际意义。

【英译文】

Once when Zi Lu, Zeng Xi, Ran You and Gong Xi Hua were seated in attendance upon the Master. The Master said, "You regard me as a man older than yourselves. Forget it for a while. As you are not employed in government you are always saying, 'Nobody knows me!' Suppose someone did employ you in government, what would you do?"

Zi Lu promptly and confidently replied, "Give me a state of a thousand war-chariots, hemmed in by big powers, or even invaded by foreign armies, and with famine at home, and in three years I will endow the people with courage and teach them to know rites."

The Master (Confucius) smiled at him.

"What would you do, Ran You?" he asked.

Ran You replied, "Give me a state of sixty to seventy or fifty to sixty square miles, and in three years I could bring the people sufficiency. But as to rites and music, I should have to leave them to a real gentleman."

"And you, Gongxi Hua?" he asked. Gongxi Hua answered, "I do not consider myself ready for office, but I should like to learn through holding one. I should like to be a junior assistant at the ancestral sacrifices or at the formal gathering of princes."

"What about you, Zeng Xi?"

The nots of the zither Zeng Xi was playing softly died away, He put his instrument down, rose, and replied, "I fear my choice will be different from that of the other three."

The Master (Confucius) said, "That doesn't matter. Each is expressing his own mind."

So Zeng Zi said, "At the end of spring, when the making of spring clothing has been completed, along with five or six young men and six or seven lads, I like to bathe in the Yi River, air myself at the Rain Dance Altar, and then return home singing."

The Master (Confucius) heaved a deep sigh and said, "I am with Zeng Xi."

When the other three left, Zeng Xi remained behind and asked, "What do you think of what the other three said?" The Master said, "Each of them was merely expressing his own mind."

"Why did you smile in the case of Zhong You?"

"A state is to be governed through the rites, but his words showed no modesty; hence I sneered at him."

"In Ran You's case there was no question of a state?" "Where have you seen a state of sixty to seventy or fifty to sixty square miles that wasn't a state?"

"Well, then, in the case of Gongxi Hua there was no state involved?" "The business of the ancestral sacrifices and formal gathering can only be undertaken by feudal princes, if Gongxi Hua were taking a minor part, who else can be capable of playing a major one?"

【英译文】

Once when Zi Lu, Zeng Xi, Ran You and Gong Xi Hua were seated in attendance upon the Master. The Master said, "You regard me as a man older than yourselves. Forget it for a while. As you are not employed in government you are always saying, 'Nobody knows me!' Suppose someone did employ you in government, what would you do?"

Zi Lu promptly and confidently replied, "Give me a state of a thousand war-chariots, hemmed in by big powers, or even invaded by foreign armies, and with famine at home, and in three years I will endow the people with courage and teach them to know rites."

The Master (Confucius) smiled at him.

"What would you do, Ran You?" he asked.

Ran You replied, "Give me a state of sixty to seventy or fifty square miles, and in three years I could bring the people sufficiency. But as to rites and music, I should have to leave them to a real gentleman."

"And you, Gongxi Hua?" he asked. Gongxi Hua answered, "I do not consider myself ready for office, but I should like to learn through holding one. I should like to be a junior assistant at the ancestral sacrifices or at the formal gathering of princes."

"What about you, Zeng Xi?"

The note of the zither Zeng Xi was playing softly died away. He put his instrument down, rose, and replied, "I fear my choice will be different from that of the other three."

The Master (Confucius) said, "That doesn't matter. Each is expressing his own mind."

So Zeng Zi said, "At the end of spring, when the making of spring clothing has been completed, along with five or six young men and six or seven lads, I like to bathe in the Yi River, air myself at the Rain Dance Altar, and then return home singing."

The Master (Confucius) heaved a deep sigh and said, "I am with Zeng Xi."

When the other three left, Zeng Xi remained behind and asked, "What do you think of what the other three said?" The Master said, "Each of them was merely expressing his own mind."

"Why did you smile in the case of Zhong You?"

"A state is to be governed through the rites, but his words showed no modesty; hence I sneered at him."

"In Ran You's case there was no question of a state?" "Where have you seen a state of sixty to seventy or fifty square miles that wasn't a state?"

"Well, then, in the case of Gongxi Hua there was no state involved?" "The business of the ancestral sacrifices and formal gathering can only be undertaken by feudal princes. If Gongxi Hua were taking a minor part, who else can be capable of playing a major one?"

颜渊篇第十二（共二十四章）

On How to Have Charity in the Heart

12.1

颜渊问仁。子曰："克己复礼为仁[1]，一日克己复礼，天下归仁焉[2]。为仁由己，而由人乎哉？"

颜渊曰："请问其目[3]。"子曰："非礼勿视，非礼勿听，非礼勿言，非礼勿动。"

颜渊曰："回虽不敏，请事斯语矣[4]。"

【中译文】

颜渊问什么是仁。孔子说："克制自己的私欲，使言行符合于'礼'，就是仁。有一天做到了克制自己的私欲，符合于礼，天下就都会崇尚'仁'了。实行仁，在于自己，难道在于别人吗？"颜渊说："请问实行仁的具体途径。"孔子说："不符合礼的不看，不符合礼的不听，不符合礼的不说，不符合礼的不做。"颜渊说："我虽然不聪敏，但我一定按照您的话去做。"

【注释】

1 克己复礼："克"，克制，约束，抑制。"己"，自己。这里指一己的私欲。"复"，回复。
2 归仁：朱熹说："归，犹与也。""一日克己复礼，则天下之人皆与其仁，极言其效之甚速而至大也。"

论语意解

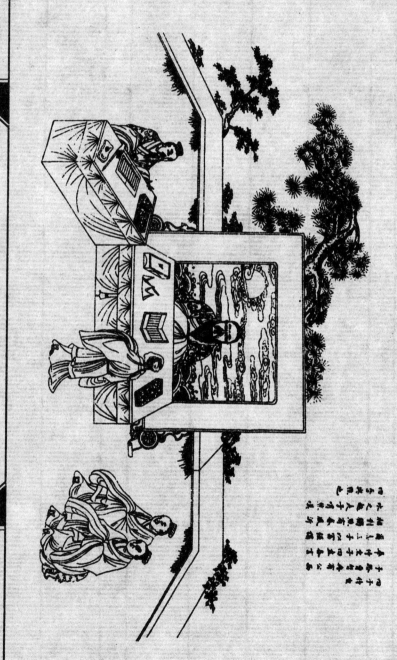

四子侍坐 Four Disciples Sitting by Confucius

顏淵篇第十二 (卷二十四章)

On How to Have Charity in the Heart

12.1

顏淵問仁。子曰:"克己復禮為仁。一日克己復禮,天下歸仁焉。為仁由己,而由人乎哉?"

顏淵曰:"請問其目。"子曰:"非禮勿視,非禮勿聽,非禮勿言,非禮勿動。"

顏淵曰:"回雖不敏,請事斯語矣。"

【中譯文】

顏淵問什么是仁。孔子說:"克制自己的私欲,使言行符合于'禮',就是仁。有一天做到了克制自己的私欲,使言行合于禮,天下就都稱許你是仁人了。實行仁,全要靠自己,難道還靠別人嗎?"顏淵說:"有問實行仁的具體途徑。"孔子說:"不符合禮的不看,不符合禮的不聽,不符合禮的不說,不符合禮的不做。"顏淵說:"我雖然不聰敏,也要一定按照您的話去做。"

【注釋】

1 克己復禮:"克","克制","約束","勝";"己",指自己一己的私欲。"復","回复"。

2 歸仁:朱熹說:"歸,猶與也。""一日克己復禮,"則天下人皆与其仁,極言其效之甚速而至大也。"

"与"，赞许，称赞。一说，"归"，归顺。这两句的意思就是："有一天做到了克制自己，符合于礼，天下就归顺于仁人了。"

3 目：纲目，条目，具体要点。

4 事：从事，实行，实践。

【英译文】

Yan Yuan asked about benevolence. The Master said, "He who can restrain himself and submit to rites is benevolent. Once he has been successful in doing so, everyone under Heaven would honor him as a benevolent man. In putting benevolence into practice, one depends on himself, not others." Yan Yuan said, "I beg to ask for the guiding principles of conduct." The Master said, "Look at nothing which is contrary to the rites; listen to nothing contrary to them; speak nothing contrary to them; and do nothing contrary to them." Yan Yuan said, "I know that I am not clever, but I shall try to put what you said into practice."

12.2

仲弓问仁[1]。子曰："出门如见大宾，使民如承大祭。己所不欲，勿施于人。在邦无怨，在家无怨。"

仲弓曰："雍虽不敏，请事斯语矣。"

【中译文】

仲弓请教什么是仁。孔子说："出门如同要接待贵宾一样恭敬，役使老百姓如同去承担重大的祭祀一样慎重。自己不愿意承受的，不要强加给别人。为国家办事没有怨恨，处理家事没有怨恨。"仲弓说："我虽然不聪敏，但一定按照您的话去做。"

【注释】

1 仲弓：冉雍，字仲弓。参阅《公冶长第五》第五章注。

【英译文】

Zhong Gong asked about Goodness. The Master said, Behave when away from home as though you were in the presence of an important guest. Deal with the common people as though you were officiating at an important sacrifice. Do not do to others what you would not like yourself. Then there will be no feelings of opposition to you, whether it is the affairs of a State that you are handling or the affairs of a Family. Zhong Gong said, I know that I am not clever, but I shall try to put into practice.

12.3

司马牛问仁[1]。子曰："仁者，其言也讱[2]。"曰："其言也讱，斯谓之仁已乎？"子曰："为之难，言之得无讱乎？"

【中译文】

司马牛问怎样是仁。孔子说："仁人，说话慎重。"司马牛说："说话慎重，就称作仁吗？"孔子说："凡

论语意解

事做起来都是困难的，说起来能不慎重吗？"

【注释】

1 司马牛：孔子的弟子。姓司马，名耕，一名犁，字子牛。宋国人。相传是宋国大夫桓魋（tuí）的弟弟。

2 讱（rèn）：言语迟钝，话难说出口，言若有忍而不易发。引申为说话十分慎重，不轻易开口。《史记·仲尼弟子列传》说司马牛"多言而躁"（饶舌话多，个性急躁），由此可见，孔子这一段话是针对司马牛"多言而躁"的毛病所提出的告诫。

【英译文】

Sima Niu asked about Goodness. The Master said, The Good man is chary of speech. Sima Niu said, So that is what is meant by Goodness-to be chary of speech? The Master said, Seeing that the doing of it is so difficult, how can one be otherwise than chary of talking about it?

12.4

司马牛问君子。子曰："君子不忧不惧。"

曰："不忧不惧，斯谓之君子已乎？"子曰："内省不疚¹，夫何忧何惧？"

【中译文】

司马牛问怎样是君子。孔子说："君子不忧愁，不畏惧。"司马牛说："不忧愁不畏惧，就称为君子了

吗？"孔子说："自己反省，问心无愧，那还忧愁什么畏惧什么？"

【注释】

1 省（xǐng）：检查，反省，检讨。疚（jiù）：对于自己的错误感到内心惭愧，痛苦不安。

【英译文】

Sima Niu asked about the meaning of the term Gentleman. The Master said, The Gentleman neither grieves nor fears. Sima Niu said, So that is what is meant by being a gentleman-neither to grieve nor to fear? The Master said, On looking within himself he finds no taint; so why should he either grieve of fear?

12.5

司马牛忧曰："人皆在兄弟，我独亡¹。"子夏曰："商闻之矣：'死生有命，富贵在天。'君子敬而无失，与人恭而有礼，四海之内，皆兄弟也。君子何患乎无兄弟也？"

【中译文】

司马牛忧伤地说："人家都有兄弟，惟独我没有。"子夏说："我听说过：'死生命中注定，富贵由天安排。'君子认真谨慎没有过失，对人恭敬而有礼貌，天下的人都是兄弟呀。君子何必忧虑没有兄弟呢？"

论语意解

曰："有耻且格。" 注释 ...

论语意解

12.3（续）

【注释】

1 讱(xìng)：谨慎。按，杨句：对于自己的错误能知而心谦惭，而遇著不忿。

【英译文】

Sima Niu asked about the meaning of the term Gentleman. The Master said, The Gentleman neither grieves nor fears. Sima Niu said, So that is what is meant by being a gentleman—neither to grieve nor to fear? The Master said, On looking within himself he finds no taint, so why should he either grieve of fear?

12.5

司马牛忧曰："人皆有兄弟，我独亡。"子
夏曰："商闻之矣：死生有命，富贵在天。
君子敬而无失，与人恭而有礼，四海之内，皆兄
弟也。君子何患乎无兄弟也？"

【中译文】

司马牛忧愁地说："人家都有兄弟，唯独我没有。"
子夏说："我听说过：'死生有命，富贵由天安排。'
君子认真谨慎没有过失，对人恭敬而有礼貌，天下的
人都是兄弟。君子何必忧愁没有兄弟呢？"

事情就不难了，但说话能不慎重吗？

【注释】

1 司马牛：孔子的弟子，复姓司马，名耕，字子牛，宋国人。相传是宋国大夫桓魋(tuí) 的弟弟。
2 讱(rèn)：言语迟钝，这里指难于出口。言语有心而不是及，引申为既有所须度，不轻易开口。
朱子列注："其言也讱"是言难而讱（谓若舌也），个也，谓
难也。由此可见，孔子认为，做好事要切切实实去做，多言而
实"，则不能陷迟出的意思。

【英译文】

Sima Niu asked about Goodness. The Master said, The Good man is chary of speech. Sima Niu said, So that is what is meant by Goodness—to be chary of speech? The Master said, Seeing that the doing of it is so difficult, how can one be otherwise than chary of talking about it?

12.4

司马牛问君子。子曰："君子不忧不惧。"
曰："不忧不惧，斯谓之君子已乎？"子
曰："内省不疚，夫何忧何惧？"

【中译文】

司马牛问怎样才是君子。孔子说："君子不忧愁，不
恐惧。"司马牛说："不忧愁不恐惧，就算得为君子了
吗？"孔子说："内心反省不感到内疚，还有什么忧愁和
恐惧呢？"

【注释】

1 我独亡：“亡”，同“无”。关于司马牛没有兄弟的感叹，传统的说法是：司马牛之兄桓魋，与有巢、子 颀、子车等在宋国作乱，失败后逃奔卫、齐、吴、鲁。司马牛虽始终未参与其兄的作乱，不赞成这种行为，但也被迫逃亡到鲁国。因此，司马牛有兄弟等于无兄弟。故发出这样的忧叹（事见《左传·哀公十四年》）。

【英译文】

Sima Niu said worriedly, Everyone else has brothers; I alone have none. Zi Xia said, I have heard this saying, 'Death and life are the decree of Heaven; wealth and rank depend upon the will of Heaven. If a gentleman attends to business and does not idle away his time, if he behaves with courtesy to others and observes the rules of ritual, then all within the Four Seas are his brothers.' How can any true gentleman worry that he is no brothers?

12.6

子张问明。子曰：“浸润之谮[1]，肤受之愬[2]，不行焉[3]，可谓明也已矣。浸润之谮，肤受之愬，不行焉，可谓远已矣[4]。”

【中译文】

子张问怎样是“明”。孔子说：“用不易察觉、潜移默化的方法进谗言，用直接了断，不容辩解的方法进行

诬告，对你行不通，就可以说是明白更可以说是看得远了。”

【注释】

1 浸润之谮：“浸（jìn）润”，水（液体）一点一滴逐渐湿润渗透进去。“谮（zèn）”，谗言，说人的坏话。浸润之谮，是说点滴而来、日积月累、好像水浸润般的诬陷中伤。

2 肤受之愬：“肤受”，皮肤上感觉到。“愬”，与谮义近，诽谤。《正义》说：“愬亦谮也，变其文耳。”肤受之愬，是说好像皮肤上感觉到疼痛般急迫切身的诽谤诬告。

3 不行：行不通。这里指不为那些暗里明里挑拔诬陷的话所迷惑，不听信谗言。

4 远：古语说：“远则明之至也。”《尚书·太甲中》说：“视远惟明，听德惟聪。”可见“远”及上句中的“明”均指看得明白，看得深远、透彻，而“远”比“明”要更进一步。

【英译文】

Zi Zhang asked how to be a wise man. The Master said, He who is influenced neither by the soaking in of slander nor by the assault of denunciation may indeed be called wise. He who is influenced neither by the soaking in of slander nor by the assault of denunciation may indeed be called 'aloof'.

【英译文】

Sima Niu said worriedly, 'Everyone else has brothers; I alone have none.' Zi Xia said, 'I have heard this saying, "Death and life are the decree of Heaven; wealth and rank depend upon the will of Heaven. If a gentleman attends to business and does not idle away his time, if he behaves with courtesy to others and observes the rules of ritual, then all within the Four Seas are his brothers.' How can any true gentleman worry that he is no brothers?"

12.6

【英译文】

Zi Zhang asked how to be a wise man. The Master said, He who is influenced neither by the soaking in of slander nor by the assault of denunciation may indeed be called wise. He who is influenced neither by the soaking in of slander nor by the assault of denunciation may indeed be called 'aloof.'

forgo? The Master said, Food. For from of old death has been the lot of all men; but without the confidence of the people there would be no government.

12.8

棘子成曰[1]："君子质而已矣[2]，何以文为[3]？"子贡曰："惜乎，夫子之说君子也！驷不及舌[4]。文犹质也，质犹文也。虎豹之鞹犹犬羊之鞹[5]。"

【中译文】

棘子成说："君子只要质朴就行了，为何还要那些文采？"子贡说："可惜呀，夫子您竟这样评说君子。君子一言，驷马难追呀！文如同质，质如同文，两者同样重要。如果不重视文采，去掉毛的虎豹皮，与去掉毛的犬羊皮就看不出有多大区别。"

【注释】

1 棘子成：卫国的大夫。

2 质：质朴，内在的思想品质、道德修养纯朴。

3 文：花纹，文采。引申为文辞、礼仪等方面的修养。

4 驷不及舌："驷(sì)"，四匹马拉的车。"舌"，指说出来的话。话一说出口，是追不回来的。

5 鞹(kuò)：同"鞟"。去掉了毛的兽皮。

【英译文】

Ji Zi Cheng said, A gentleman is a gentleman in virtue of the stuff he is made

---

论语意解

二九八　二九七

12.7

子贡问政。子曰："足食，足兵[1]，民信之矣。"子贡曰："必不得已而去，于斯三者何先？"曰："去兵。"子贡曰："必不得已而去，于斯二者何先？"曰："去食。自古皆有死，民无信不立。"

【中译文】

子贡问怎样治理国家。孔子说："有充足的粮食，有充足的军备，引导人民信任政府。"子贡说："不得已一定要去掉一项，在这三项中哪一项先去掉呢？"孔子说："去掉军备。"子贡说："不得已一定要再去掉一项，在剩下的这两项中去掉哪一项呢？"孔子说："去掉粮食。自古以来人都是要死的，但如果人民政府不信任，政府就维持不住。"

【注释】

1 兵：兵器，武器。这里指军备。

【英译文】

Zi Gong asked about government. The Master said, Sufficient food, sufficient weapons, and the confidence of the common people. Zi Gong said, Suppose you had no choice the but to dispense with one of these three, which would you forgo? The Master said, Weapons. Zi Gong said, Suppose you were forced to dispense with one of the two that were left, which would you

论语译解

12.7

子贡问政。子曰："足食，足兵，民信之矣。"子贡曰："必不得已而去，于斯三者何先？"曰："去兵。"子贡曰："必不得已而去，于斯二者何先？"曰："去食。自古皆有死，民无信不立。"

【中译文】

子贡问怎样治理国家。孔子说："有充足的粮食，有充足的军备，让人民信任政府。"子贡说："不得已一定要去一项，在这三项中哪一项先去掉呢？"孔子说："去掉军备。"子贡说："不得已一定要再去掉一项，在剩下的两项中去掉哪一项呢？"孔子说："去掉粮食。自古以来人都是要死的，但如果人民政府不信任，就没有国家了。"

【注释】

1. 兵：兵器、军器，这里指军备。

【英译文】

Zi Gong asked about government. The Master said, Sufficient food, sufficient weapons, and the confidence of the common people. Zi Gong said, Suppose you had no choice the but to dispense with one of these three, which would you forgo? The Master said, Weapons. Zi Gong said, Suppose you were forced to dispense with one of the two that were left, which would you forgo? The Master said, Food. For from of old death has been the lot of all men, but without the confidence of the people there would be no government.

12.8

棘子成曰："君子质而已矣，何以文为？"子贡曰："惜乎，夫子之说君子也！驷不及舌。文犹质也，质犹文也。虎豹之鞟犹犬羊之鞟。"

【中译文】

棘子成说："君子只要质朴就行了，为何还要做那些文采？"子贡说："可惜啊！您这样谈论君子，四匹马拉的车也追不上您的舌头。两者同样重要。如果不重视文采，去掉毛的虎豹皮，和去掉毛的犬羊皮就没有什么区别了。"

【注释】

1. 棘子成：卫国的大夫。
2. 质：朴。内有的思想品质，道德修养等等。
3. 文：花纹、文采。引申为文辞，孔子以学习而而修养。
4. 驷不及舌："驷"(sì)："四匹马拉的车","舌"：指说出来的话。话，说出口，是追不回来的。
5. 鞟(kuò)：同"鞹"。去掉了毛的兽皮。

【英译文】

Ji Zi Cheng said, A gentleman is a gentleman in virtue of the stuff he is made.

税制度。就是国家从耕地的收获中抽取十分之一作为田税。

3 二：指国家从耕地的收获中抽取十分之二作为田税。鲁国自宣公十五年（公元前594年）起，不再实行"彻"法，而是以"二"抽税。

【英译文】

Duke Ai asked You Ruo, "What is to be done when it is a year of famine and our supplies are insufficient?" You Ruo replied, "Why not levy a tax of one-tenth?" The Duke said, "I find a tax of two-tenths insufficient, so how can we follow your suggestion?" You Ruo said, "When the people have sufficiency, how can the prince fail to have enough? If the people do not have sufficiency, how can the prince have enough?"

12.10

子张问崇德辨惑。子曰："主忠信，徙义[1]，崇德也。爱之欲其生，恶之欲其死，既欲其生，又欲其死，是惑也。'诚不以富，亦只以异[2]'。"

【中译文】

子张问怎样推崇仁德，辨别迷惑。孔子说："以忠诚信实为主，行为以义为指导，就是推崇仁德。喜爱一个人就希望他永远活着，厌恶起来又恨不得让他马上死去，既要他活，又要他死，就是迷惑。

【注释】

1 徙义：指向义迁移、靠拢，按照义去做。"徙（xǐ）"，

of. Culture cannot make gentlemen. Zi Gong said, I am sorry. That you should have said that, For the saying goes that 'when a gentleman has spoken, a team of four horses cannot overtake his words'. Culture is just as important as inborn qualities; and inborn qualities, no less important than culture. Remove the hairs from the skin of a tiger of panther, and What is left looks just like the hairless hide of a dog or sheep.

12.9

哀公问于有若曰[1]："年饥，用不足，如之何？"有若对曰："盍彻乎[2]？"曰："二[3]，吾犹不足，如之何其彻也？"对曰："百姓足，君孰与不足？百姓不足，君孰与足？"

【中译文】

鲁哀公问有若："年成不好有饥荒，钱不够，怎么办呢？"有若回答说："为何不实行抽取十分之一的'彻'税法呢？"哀公说："抽十分之二的田税，我还不够用，如何能实行'彻'税法呢？"有若说："百姓富足了，您怎么会不足？百姓不富足，您怎么会富足？"

【注释】

1 哀公：鲁国国君。参阅《为政篇第二》第十九章注。有若：姓有，名若，字子有。被后人尊称"有子"。参阅《学而篇第一》第二章注。

2 盍（hé）：何不，为什么不。彻：西周的一种田

of Culture cannot make gentleman. Zi Gong said, 'I am sorry... That you should have said that. For the saying goes that when a gentleman has spoken, a team of four horses cannot overtake his words. Culture is just as important as inborn qualities, and inborn qualities, no less important than culture. Remove the hairs from the skin of a tiger of panther, and What is left looks just like the hairless hide of a dog or sheep.

12.9

论语意释

【英译文】

Duke Ai asked You Ruo, "What is to be done when it is a year of famine and our supplies are insufficient?" You Ruo replied, "Why not levy a tax of one-tenth?" The Duke said, "I find a tax of two-tenths insufficient, so how can we follow your suggestion?" You Ruo said, "When the people have sufficiency, how can the prince fail to have enough? If the people do not have sufficiency, how can the prince have enough?"

12.10

【注 释】

1 齐景公：姓姜，名杵臼（chǔ jiù）。齐庄公异母弟。公元前547－公元前490年在位。鲁昭公末年孔子到齐国时，齐大夫陈氏权势日重，而齐景公爱奢侈，多内嬖，厚赋敛，施重刑，不立太子，不听从晏婴的劝谏，国内政治混乱。所以，当齐景公问政时，孔子作了以上的回答。景公虽然口头上赞许同意孔子的　意见，却未能真正采纳实行，为君而不尽君道，后来齐国终于被陈氏篡夺。

【英译文】

Duke Jing of Qi asked the Master about government. The Master replied, Let the prince be a prince, the minister a minister, the father a father and the son a son. The Duke said, How true! For indeed when the prince is not a prince, the minister not a minister, the father not a father, the son not a son, one may have a dish of millet in front of one and yet not know if one will live to eat it.

12. 12

子曰："片言可以折狱者[1]，其由也与！"子路无宿诺[2]。

【中译文】

孔子说："根据人的只言片语，就可以断案的，大概只有仲由吧！"子路没有过夜而不兑现的诺言。

迁移。

2 "诚不以富"，"亦只以异"，此处是错简、不译。

【英译文】

Zi Zhang asked what was meant by 'piling up moral force' and 'deciding when in two minds' The Master said, 'by piling up moral force' is meant taking loyalty and good faith as one's guiding principles, and migrating to places where right prevails. Again, to love a thing means wanting it to live, to hate a thing means wanting it to perish. But suppose I want something to live and at the same time want it to perish; that is 'being in two minds'. Not for her wealth, But merely for a change.

12. 11

齐景公问政于孔子[1]，孔子对曰："君君，臣臣，父父，子子。"公曰："善哉！信如君不君，臣不臣，父不父，子不子，虽有粟，吾得而食诸？"

【中译文】

齐景公向孔子求教如何治理国家，孔子回答说："君要像君的样子，臣要像臣的样子，父要像父的样子，子要像子的样子。"齐景公说："很好啊！果真是君不像君，臣不像臣，父不像父，子不像子，虽然有粮食，我能吃得到吗？"

论语篇解

【注释】

1. 齐景公：姓姜，名杵臼（chǔ jiù），齐君，公元前547—公元前490年在位。曾向孔子预问政。当时齐大夫陈氏权势日重，齐景公要姑息之以为荣，厚敛渔，施重赋，不立太子，不听从晏婴的劝谏，国内政混乱。因此，当齐景公问政时，孔子才以主臣的回答。最后虽然君王赞有同意孔子的意见，却未能真正采纳实行，以至而不久寿道，后来齐国终于被陈氏篡夺。

【英译文】

Duke Jing of Qi asked the Master about government. The Master replied, Let the prince be a prince, the minister a minister, the father a father and the son a son. The Duke said, How true! For indeed when the prince is not a prince, the minister not a minister, the father not a father, the son not a son, one may have a dish of millet in front of one and yet not know if one will live to eat it.

12.12

子曰："片言可以折狱者，其由也与？"子路无宿诺。

【中译文】

孔子说："听讼人的只言片语，就可以断案的，大概只有由吧。"子路没有过夜而不兑现的话言。

【注释】

1. 片言：即片面之辞，也就是诉讼双方中一方的言辞。
2. 宿不以诺：一说其以宿；此处是借简，一不注。

【英译文】

Zi Zhang asked what was meant by 'piling up moral force' and 'deciding when in two minds.' The Master said, 'by piling up moral force' is meant taking loyalty and good faith as one's guiding principles, and migrating to places where right prevails. Again, to love a thing means wanting it to live, to hate a thing means wanting it to perish. But suppose I want something to live and at the same time want it to perish; that is being in two minds. Not for her wealth, But merely for a change.

12.11

齐景公问政于孔子。孔子对曰："君君，臣臣，父父，子子。"公曰："善哉！信如君不君，臣不臣，父不父，子不子，虽有粟，吾得而食诸？"

【中译文】

齐景公向孔子来请教如何治理国家。孔子回答说："君是像君的样子，臣是像臣的样子，父是像父的样子，子是像子的样子。"齐景公说："说得对！如果真是君不像君，臣不像臣，父不像父，子不像子，虽然有粮食，我能够吃到吗？"

12.14

子张问政。子曰："居之无倦，行之以忠。"

【中译文】

子张问怎样从政。孔子说："坚守职位不松懈，执行政令要忠实。"

【英译文】

Zi Zhang asked about public business. The Master said, Ponder over it untiringly at home; carry it out loyally when the time comes.

12.15

子曰："博学于文，约之以礼，亦可以弗畔矣夫[1]！"

【中译文】

孔子说："广泛地多学文化典籍，用礼来约束自己，就可以不违背君子之道了吧！"

【注释】

1 本章与《雍也篇第六》第二十七章文字略同，可参阅。

论语意解

【注释】

1 片言：指原告被告诉讼双方中一方的片面言辞。"片"，单方面的。折：断，判断，区别是非曲直。狱：讼事，案件。

2 无宿诺：没有过宿隔夜的诺言，没有拖延而不实现的许诺。"宿"，隔夜。

【英译文】

The Master (Confucius) said, Talk about 'deciding a lawsuit with half a word' -Zhong You is the man for that. Zi Lu never slept over a promise.

12.13

子曰："听讼[1]，吾犹人也，必也使无讼乎！"

【中译文】

孔子说："谈到处理诉讼，我同别人一样，但重要的是能使诉讼消失在萌芽状态。"

【注释】

1 听讼：处理诉讼。"听"，判断，审理，处理。

【英译文】

The Master (Confucius) said, I could try a civil suit as well as anyone. But better still to bring it about that there were no civil suits!

12.14

子张问政。子曰："居之无倦，行之以忠。"

【中译文】

子张问怎样治政。孔子说："居于官位不懈怠，执行政令要忠实。"

【英译文】

Zi Zhang asked about public business. The Master said, 'Ponder over it untiringly at home; carry it out loyally when the time comes.'

12.15

子曰："博学于文，约之以礼，亦可以弗畔矣夫！"

【中译文】

孔子说："广泛地学习文化典籍，用礼来约束自己，这就可以不违背君子之道了罢！"

【注释】

1 本章与《雍也篇第六》第二十七章文字略同，可参阅。

【注释】

1 片言：指诉讼双方在诉论中一方的片面言辞。"言"，单方面的。折：断；判断。以判断非曲直。
雄：必事，案件。
2 无宿诺：没有立刻履行的诺言。旧有隔宿而不实现，即拖欠。"宿"，隔夜。

【英译文】

The Master (Confucius) said, 'Talk about deciding a lawsuit with half a word. Zhong You is the man for that. Zi Lu never slept over a promise.'

12.13

子曰："听讼，吾犹人也，必也使无讼乎！"

【中译文】

孔子说："审理诉讼案件，我同别人一样，但重要的是必须使诉讼案件根本不发生才好。"

【注释】

1 听讼：处理诉讼。"听"，判断，审理。讼，诉讼。

【英译文】

The Master (Confucius) said, 'I could by a civil suit as well as anyone. But better still to bring it about that there were no civil suits!'

【英译文】

Ji Kangzi asked the Master about the art of ruling. The Master said, Ruling is straightening. If you lead along a straight way, who will dare to do otherwise?

12. 18

季康子患盗，问于孔子。孔子对曰："苟子之不欲[1]，虽赏之不窃。"

【中译文】

季康子担忧盗贼多。向孔子询问对策。孔子回答说："假如您不重财货，就是奖励盗窃，也没有人去盗窃。"

【注释】

1 苟（gǒu）：假如，如果。

【英译文】

Ji Kangzi was troubled by robbers. He asked the Master what he should do. The Master replied, If only you were free from desire, they would not steal even if you paid them to.

12. 19

季康子问政于孔子曰："如杀无道，以就有道，何如？"孔子对曰："子为政，焉用杀？子欲善而民善矣。君子之德风，小人之德草，草

论语意解

【英译文】

The Master (Confucius) said, "One who is widely versed in letters and at the same time knows how to submit his learning to the restraints of rites doesn't turn to go far wrong."

12. 16

子曰："君子成人之美，不成人之恶。小人反是。"

【中译文】

孔子说："君子成全别人的好事，不帮别人做成坏事。小人则与此相反。"

【英译文】

The Master (Confucius) said, "A gentleman enables the good wishes of others, not the bad ones. A petty man does just the reverse of this."

12. 17

季康子问政于孔子。孔子对曰："政者，正也。子师以正，孰敢不正？"

【中译文】

季康子向孔子请教如何从政。孔子回答说："政，就是正。您领头端正自己，谁敢不端正自己？"

【英译文】

The Master (Confucius) said, "One who is widely versed in letters and at the same time knows how to submit his learning to the restraints of rites doesn't turn to far wrong."

12.16

子曰："君子成人之美，不成人之恶。小人反是。"

【中译文】

孔子说："君子成全别人的好事，不促成别人的坏事。小人却与此相反。"

【英译文】

The Master (Confucius) said, "A gentleman enables the good wishes of others, not the bad ones. A petty man does just the reverse of this."

12.17

季康子问政于孔子。孔子对曰："政者，正也。子帅以正，孰敢不正？"

【中译文】

季康子向孔子请教如何治政。孔子答道："政就是正的意思。您自己带头走正路，谁敢不走正道呢？"

【英译文】

Ji Kangzi asked the Master about the art of ruling. The Master said, "Ruling is straightening. If you lead along a straight way, who will dare to do otherwise?"

12.18

季康子患盗，问于孔子。孔子对曰："苟子之不欲，虽赏之不窃。"

【中译文】

季康子因盗窃成患，向孔子询问对策。孔子对答道："假如您自己不贪求财货，即使有人去奖赏偷窃，他们也不会干。"

【注释】

1 苟（gǒu）：假如，如果。

【英译文】

Ji Kangzi was troubled by robbers. He asked the Master what he should do. The Master replied, "If only you were free from desire, they would not steal even if you paid them to."

12.19

季康子问政于孔子曰："如杀无道，以就有道，何如？"孔子对曰："子为政，焉用杀？子欲善而民善矣。君子之德风，小人之德草，草上之风，必偃。"

直而好义，察言而观色，虑以下人。在邦必达，在家必达。夫闻也者，色取仁而行违，居之不疑。在邦必闻，在家必闻。”

【中译文】

子张问：“知识分子如何才叫作‘达’？”孔子说：“你所说的‘达’指什么？”子张回答说：“在朝廷做官一定有名声，宗族中一定有名声。”孔子说：“这只是名声，而不是‘达’。所谓‘达’的人，要质朴正直，讲究礼义，善于分析别人的言语，观察别人的脸色，经常想着对人谦恭有礼貌。这样的人在朝廷做官一定‘达’，在宗族中也一定‘达’。至于有虚名的人，表面上好像主张仁德，行动上却违反仁德，还以仁人自居而不怀疑。这样的人也会在朝廷和宗族中赢得名声。”

【注释】

1 达：通达，显达，处事通情达理，做官地位显贵。孔子认为，达者必须质直好义，具有仁德与智慧，才能与官职地位名实相副。

2 闻：有名声，名望。这里指虚有其名，名实不副。“闻”与“达”相似，而本质不同。达重在诚，要务实，自修于内，闻旨在伪，外求虚名，欺世盗名。

【英译文】

Zi Zhang asked, In what conditions a gentleman could be said to have

---

论语意解

三〇八

三〇七

上之风[1]，必偃[2]。”

【中译文】

季康子向孔子询问如何为政，说：“如果杀恶人，亲近好人，怎样？”孔子回答说：“您为政，怎么还用杀人呢？您要是想做好事，百姓也会做好事的。君子的品德就像风，小人的品德就像草，风吹草上，草必然随风倒下。”

【注释】

1 草上之风：指草上有风，风吹到草上。

2 偃（yǎn）：扑倒，倒下。

【英译文】

Ji Kangzi asked the Master about government, saying, Suppose I were to slay those who have not the Way in order to help on those who have the Way, what would you think of it? The Master replied, You are there to rule, not to slay. If you desire what is good, the people will at once be good. The essence of the gentleman is that of wind; the essence of small people is that of grass. And when a wind passes over the grass, it cannot choose but bend.

12.20

子张问：“士何如斯可谓之达矣[1]？”子曰：“何哉，尔所谓达者？”子张对曰：“在邦必闻[2]，在家必闻。”子曰：“是闻也，非达也。夫达也者，质

【英译文】

Ji Kangzi asked the Master about government, saying, Suppose I were to slay those who have not the Way in order to help on those who have the Way, what would you think of it? The Master replied, You are there to rule, not to slay. If you desire what is good, the people will at once be good. The essence of the gentleman is that of wind: the essence of small people is that of grass. And when a wind passes over the grass, it cannot choose but bend.

12.20

子张问："士何如斯可谓之达矣？"子曰："何哉，尔所谓达者？"子张对曰："在邦必闻，在家必闻。"子曰："是闻也，非达也。夫达也者，质

【英译文】

Zi Zhang asked, In what conditions a gentleman could be said to have

就是糊涂吗？"

【注 释】

1 修：整治，消除改正。慝(tè)：邪恶的念头。

【英译文】

Once when Fan Chi was having a walk with the Master at the site of the Rain Dance Altars, he asked about how to enhance one's virtue, correct one's mistakes, and tell the true from the false. The Master said, "What excellent questions! Consider your job of prime importance and put the reward in second place, isn't that enhancing virtue? Attack the evil within yourself and do not attack the evil in others, isn't that correcting one's mistakes? In a burst of anger to forget one's safety and that of one's family, isn't that utter confusion?"

12.22

樊迟问仁。子曰："爱人。"问知[1]。子曰："知人。"

樊迟未达[2]。子曰："举直错诸枉[3]，能使枉者直。"

樊迟退，见子夏曰："乡也[4]，吾见于夫子而问知，子曰：'举直错诸枉，能使枉者直。'何谓也？"

子夏曰："富哉言乎！舜有天下，选于众，举皋陶[5]，不仁者远矣[6]。汤有天下[7]，选于众，举伊尹[8]，不仁者远矣。"

论语意解

三一〇九

shown good sense. The Master said, "That depends on what you mean by being sensible?" Zi Zhang replied, saying, "If employed by the state, one is certain to win fame; if employed by a senior official, one is certain to win fame." The Master (Confucius) said, "That describes being famous; it does not describe being sensible. The one who has shown good sense must be by nature upright and fond of justice. He must examine men's words and observe their expressions, and bear in mind the necessity of deferring to others. Such a man, whether employed by the state or by a senior official, will certainly be sensible. The man who wins fame may have obtained, by his outward airs, a reputation for morality, which his conduct quite belies. However he claims that with sufficient self-assurance. Such a man is certain to win fame by deception whether employed by the state or by a senior official. "

12.21

樊迟从游于舞雩之下，曰："敢问崇德，修慝[1]，辨惑。"子曰："善哉问！先事后得，非崇德与？攻其恶，无攻人之恶，非修慝与？一朝大忿，忘其身，以及其亲，非惑与？"

【中译文】

樊迟陪着孔子出游于舞雩台下，问孔子："怎样推崇仁德？怎样消除邪念？怎样辨清迷惑？"孔子说："问得好！首先努力去做该做的事，不计较后来得到的收获，不就是推崇仁德么？改掉自己的错误，不攻击别人的错误，不就是消除邪念么？忍不住一时的气愤，而忘掉自身安危，甚至连累自己的父母亲的人，不

崇德辨惑

【注释】

1. 慝：藏恶。崇德：提高道德。 慝(tè)：邪恶的念头。

【译文】

Once when Fan Chi was having a walk with the Master at the site of the Rain Dance Altars, he asked about how to enhance one's virtue, correct one's mistakes, and tell the true from the false. The Master said, "What excellent questions! Consider your job of prime importance and put the reward in second place, isn't that enhancing virtue? Attack the evil within yourself and do not attack the evil in others, isn't that correcting one's mistakes? In a burst of anger to forget one's safety and that of one's family, isn't that utter confusion?"

12.22

樊迟问仁。子曰："爱人。"问知。子曰："知人。"

樊迟未达。子曰："举直错诸枉，能使枉者直。"

樊迟退，见子夏曰："乡也，吾见于夫子而问知，子曰：'举直错诸枉，能使枉者直。'何谓也？"

子夏曰："富哉言乎！舜有天下，选于众，举皋陶，不仁者远矣。汤有天下，选于众，举伊尹，不仁者远矣。"

【中译文】

樊迟问怎么才能是仁爱于人。孔子说："爱护体谅他人。"又问怎样才是明智？孔子说："了解人。"樊迟还不能理解。孔子又说："把正直的人提拔起来，使他们的位置在邪恶的人之上，就可以使邪恶的人也正直起来。"樊迟辞别孔子出来，见到子夏，

12.21

欲显扬士君子之才德，曰："崇何德？非一恶？以其惑，不以人之恶，非一朝一夕矣，志先悲，以反其亲，非惑与？"

【中文名】

刑法。

6 远：疏远，远离。

7 汤：商朝开国君主，名履，灭夏桀而得天下。

8 伊尹：名挚，汤任他为"阿衡"（即宰相），曾辅助汤灭夏兴商。

【英译文】

Fan Chi asked about benevolence, the Master said, "To love men." He asked about wisdom, the Mater said, "To know men." Since Fan Chi did not quite understand, the Master continued, "If you will put upright persons above the crooked, you will be making the crooked straight." Then Fan Chi withdrew and reported the conversation to Zi Xia. "What did our Master mean?" asked Fan Chi.

Zi Xia said, "Meaningful indeed are those words of his! When Shun ruled the world, he made his selection from the many and chose Gao Yao, and the crooked disappeared. When Tang, founder of the Yin Dynasty, ruled the world, he, too, made his selection from the many and chose Yi Yin, and the crooked disappeared."

12.23

子贡问友。子曰："忠告而善道之[1]，不可则止，毋自辱焉[2]。"

【中译文】

子贡问怎样对待朋友。孔子说："要忠诚地劝告他，委婉恰当地开导他，他还不听从，就停止算了，不要

论语意解

【中译文】

樊迟问什么是仁。孔子说："爱人。"樊迟又问什么是智。孔子说："知道识别人。"樊迟还不能透彻理解。孔子说："推举选拔正直的人，安排在邪恶的人之上，这样就能使邪恶的人转化为正直。"樊迟从孔子那儿退出来，见到子夏，说："刚才我见到老师，问什么是智，老师说：'选拔推举正直的人，安排在邪恶的人之上，这样就能使邪恶的人转化为正直。'这话是什么意思呀？"子夏说："这是意义丰富而深刻的话啊！舜有了天下，在众人中选拔人才，推举了皋陶，不仁的人就被疏远了。汤有了天下，在众人中选拔人才，推举了伊尹，不仁的人就被疏远了。"

【注释】

1 知：通"智"。

2 未达：还没明白，没透彻理解。"仁"是"爱人"，不分亲疏远近都要爱；而"智"又要求知道了解人，善于识别人，辨明正、邪、贤、否、智、愚而区别对待；那么，"仁"与"智"是否矛盾，要做到"智"是否会妨害"仁"？樊迟心里含糊，弄不大通，故说"未达"。

3 错诸枉：置于邪恶的人之上。参见《为政篇第二》第十九章注。

4 乡：通"向"。从前。此犹说"刚才"。

5 皋陶（gāoyáo）：传说舜时大臣，任"士师"，掌管

【英译文】

Fan Chi asked about benevolence, the Master said, "To love men." He asked about wisdom, the Mater said, "To know men." Since Fan Chi did not quite understand, the Master continued, "If you will put upright persons above the crooked, you will be making the crooked straight." Then Fan Chi withdrew and reported the conversation to Zi Xia, "What did our Master mean?" asked Fan Chi.

Zi Xia said, "Meaningful indeed are those words of his! When Shun ruled the world, he made his selection from the many and chose Gao Yao, and the crooked disappeared. When Tang, founder of the Yin Dynasty, ruled the world, he, too, made his selection from the many and chose Yi Yin, and the crooked disappeared."

12.23

【中译文】

自招侮辱。"

【注释】

1 道：同"导"。引导，诱导。

2 毋（wú）：勿，不要。

【英译文】

　　Zi Gong asked about friends. The Master said, inform them loyally and guide them discreetly. If that fails, then desist. Do not go so far as to disgrace yourself.

12.24

　　曾子曰："君子以文会友，以友辅仁。"

【中译文】

　　曾子说："君子通过文章学问来结交朋友，依靠朋友的帮助来辅助仁德。"

【英译文】

　　Zeng Zi said, A gentleman by his culture collects friends about him, and through these friends promotes Goodness.

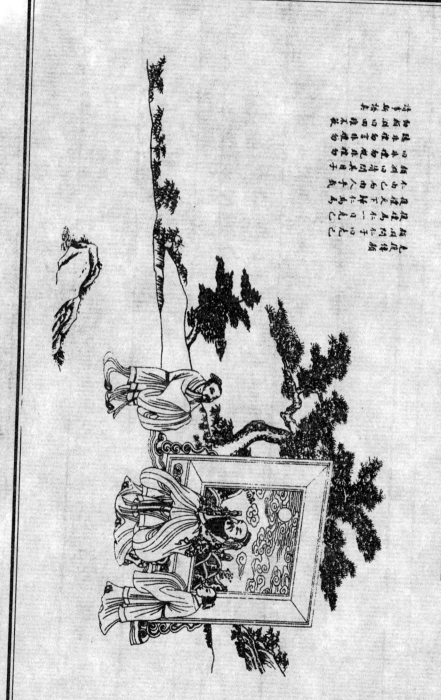

克复传颜　Teaching Self-Control and Ritual to Yan Yuan

论语意解

Leeching Sense-Out and Ritual to Lun Yuan

子贡问友。子曰："忠告而善道之，不可则止，毋自辱焉。"

【注释】
1. 道：同"导"，引导，劝导。
2. 固（wǔ）：辱，羞辱。

【英译文】
Zi Gong asked about friends. The Master said, inform them loyally and guide them discreetly. If that fails, then desist. Do not go so far as to disgrace yourself.

12.24

曾子曰："君子以文会友，以友辅仁。"

【中译文】
曾子说："君子通过文章学习来结交朋友，依靠朋友的帮助培养仁德。"

【英译文】
Zeng Zi said, A gentleman collects friends about him, and through these friends promotes Goodness.

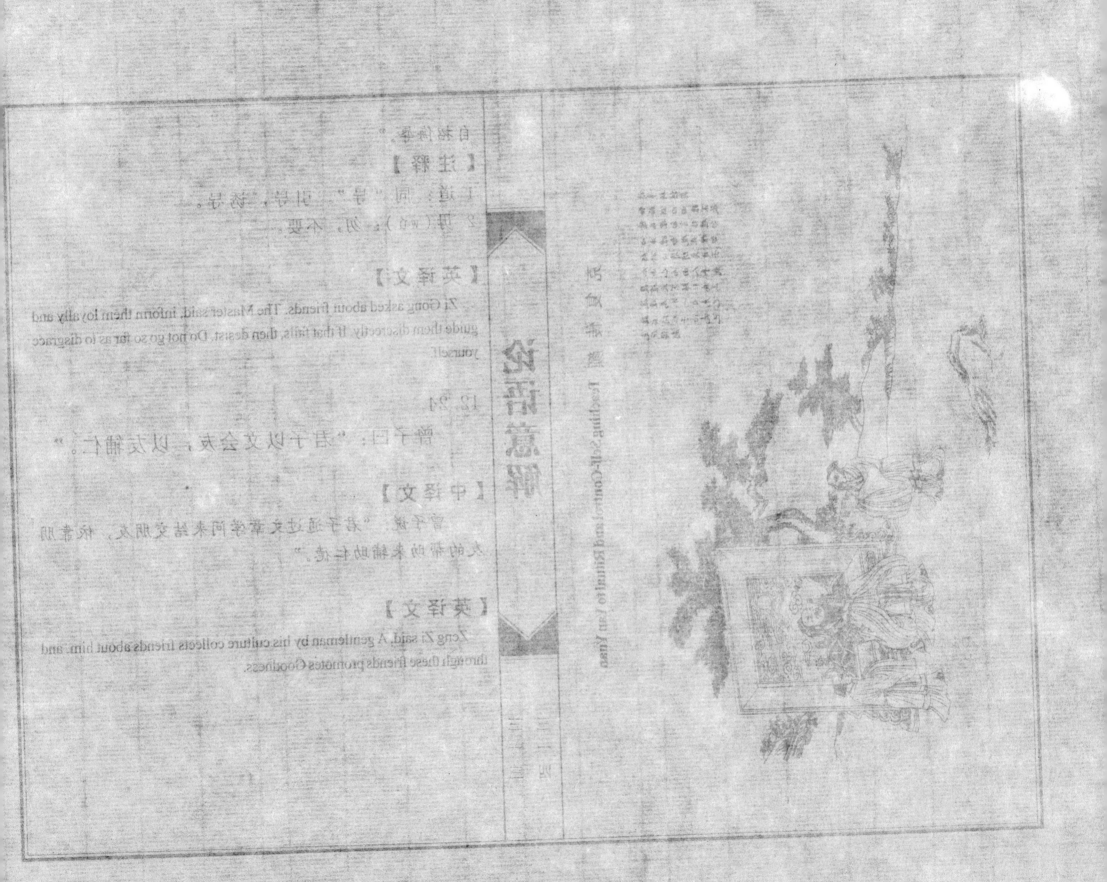

子路篇第十三（共三十章）

Confucius Teaching His Students How to Be a Good Person

13.1

子路问政。子曰："先之[1]，劳之[2]。"请益。曰："无倦。"

【中译文】

子路问如何从政。孔子说："自先士卒，不怕劳累以为示范。"子路请求多讲一点。孔子说："永远不要松懈怠惰。"

【注释】

1 先之：指为政者身体力行，凡事率先垂范，以身作则。"之"，代词，指百姓。

2 劳之：这里指为政者亲身去干，以自身的"先劳"，带动老百姓都勤劳地干，虽勤而无怨。

【英译文】

Zi Lu asked about government. The Master said, Lead them; encourage them! Zi Lu asked for a further maxim. The Master said, Work Untiringly.

13.2

仲弓为季氏宰，问政。子曰："先有司，赦小过，举贤才。"

曰："焉知贤才而举之？"子曰："举尔所知；尔所不知，人其舍诸[1]？"

【中译文】

仲弓担任季氏的总管，问怎样为政。孔子说："凡事给部下们带个好头，宽容他们的小错误，推举贤良的人才。"仲弓说："怎么能知道谁是贤才而选拔他们呢？"孔子说："选拔你所知道的；你所不知道的，别人难道会不推举他吗？"

【注释】

1 舍：舍弃，放弃。这里指不推举。诸："之乎"二字合音。

【英译文】

Zhong Gong, having become steward of the Ji Family, asked about government. The Master said, Get as much as possible done first by your subordinates. Forgive their minor mistakes. Promote men of superior capacity. Zhong Gong said, How does one know a man of superior capacity, in order to promote him? The Master said, Promote those you know, and those whom you do not know other people will certainly not neglect.

13.3

子路曰："卫君待子而为政[1]，子将奚先[2]？"子曰："必也正名乎[3]！"

子路篇第十三 （第十三章）

Confucius Teaching His Students How to Be a Good Person

13.1

子路问政。子曰:"先之,劳之。"请益。曰:"无倦。"

【中译文】

子路问如何从政,孔子说:"自己带头,走在老百姓前面……"子路请求再多讲一点。孔子说:"永远不要松懈怠倦。"

【注释】

1. 先之:带头而身体力行,其事率先而做,以身作则。"之",代而。
2. 劳之:在里指为政者要身先士卒,以自身的劳苦……带动着百姓勤劳苦干,勤勉而恳。

【英译文】

Zilu asked about government. The Master said, Lead them; encourage them. Zilu asked for a further maxim. The Master said, Work Untiringly.

13.2

仲弓为季氏宰,问政。子曰:"先有司,赦小过,举贤才。"

【中译文】

仲弓做季孙氏的家臣,向孔子请教如何处理政事。孔子说:"先给下属各个职务,责备他们的小错误,推举贤能的人才。"仲弓又问:"怎么知道谁是贤才而选拔他们呢?"孔子回答道:"你所不知道的,别人难道会不推荐吗?"

【注释】

1. 有司:官吏。古代,担任具体职务的官吏,称:"之吏"。
二,官吏的。

【英译文】

Zhong Gong, having become steward of the Ji Family, asked about government. The Master said, Get as much as possible done first by your subordinates. Forgive their minor mistakes. Promote men of superior capacity. Zhong Gong said, How does one know a man of superior capacity, in order to promote him? The Master said, Promote those you know, and those whom you do not know other people will certainly not neglect.

13.3

子路曰:"卫君待子而为政,子将奚先?"

子曰:"必也正名乎!"

子路曰："有是哉，子之迂也⁴，奚其正？"

子曰："野哉，由也！君子于其所不知，盖阙如也⁵。名不正则言不顺，言不顺则事不成，事不成则礼乐不兴，礼乐不兴则刑罚不中⁶，刑罚不中则民无所错手足⁷。故君子名之必可言也，言之必可行也。君子于其言，无所苟而已矣⁸。"

【中译文】

子路对孔子说："假如卫国国君等您去治理国家，您将先做什么事呢？"孔子说："必须先正名分吧。"子路说："有这样做的吗？您太迂了，为什么要正名分呢？"孔子说："真粗野啊，仲由！君子对自己所不知道的事情，大概总得抱着存疑的态度吧。如果名分不正，说话就不管用；说话不管用，事情就办不成；事情办不成，礼乐得不到重视；礼乐得不到重视，刑罚的执行就不会恰当；刑罚执行不恰当，人民就手足失措。所以，君子名分赋予了说话的权利，说了也一定可以办得到。君子对自己所说的话，绝不草率马虎。"

【注释】

1 卫君：卫出公蒯辄。他与父亲争位，引起国内混乱。所以孔子主张，要治理卫国，必先"正名"，以明确"君君臣臣父父子子"的关系。参阅《述而篇第七》第十五章注。

2 奚：何，什么。

3 正名：纠正礼制名分上的用词不当，正确地确定某个人的名分。"正"，纠正，改正。"名"，名分，礼制上的人的名义、身份、地位、等级等。

4 迂（yū）：迂腐；拘泥守旧，不切实际。

5 阙如：存疑；对还没搞清楚的疑难问题暂时搁置，不下判断；对缺乏确凿根据的事，不武断，不妄说。"阙"，同"缺"。

6 中（zhòng）：得当，恰当，适合。

7 错：同"措"。放置，安排，处置。

8 苟（gǒu）：苟且，随便，马虎。

【英译文】

Zi Lu said, If the prince of Wei were waiting for you to come and administer his state for him, what would be your first measure? The Master said, It would certainly be to correct language. Zi Lu said, Can I have heard you aright? Surely what you say has nothing to do with the matter. Why should language be corrected? The Master said, How rude you are! A gentleman, should maintain an attitude of reserve, When things he does not understand are mentioned. If language is incorrect, then what is said does not concord with what was meant; and if what is said does not concord with what was meant, what is to be done cannot be effected. If what is to be done cannot be effected, then rites and music will not flourish. If rites and music do not flourish, then mutilations and lesser punishments will go astray. And if mutilations and lesser punishments go astray, then the people have nowhere to put hand or foot.

Therefore the gentleman uses only such language as is proper for speech, and only speaks of what it would be proper to carry into effect. In regard to his language, a gentleman leaves nothing to mere chance.

论语意解

【英译文】

Zi Lu said, If the prince of Wei were waiting for you to come and administer his state for him, what would be your first measure? The Master said, It would certainly be to rectify language. Zi Lu said, Can! I have heard you angling? Surely what you say has nothing to do with the matter. Why should language be corrected? The Master said, How rude you are! A gentleman, should maintain an attitude of reserve. When things he does not understand are mentioned. If language is incorrect, then what is said does not concord with what was meant; and if what is said does not concord with what was meant, what is to be done cannot be effected. If what is to be done cannot be effected, then rites and music will not flourish. If rites and music do not flourish, then mutilations and lesser punishments will go astray. And if mutilations and lesser punishments go astray, then the people have nowhere to put hand or foot. Therefore the gentleman uses only such language as is proper for speech, and only speaks of what it would be proper to carry into effect. In regard to his language, a gentleman leaves nothing to mere chance.

【英译文】

Fan Chi asked the Master to teach him about farming. The Master said, "You had better consult some old farmer." He asked about gardening. The Master said, "You had better ask some old vegetable-gardener."

When Fan Chi left, the Master said, "Fan is no gentleman! When those at the top love the rites, the people won't fail to be respectful; when justice is observed at the top, the people will be obedient; when sincerity reigns at the top, the people will be honest. Then, when such a situation prevails, people will flock to him from all sides with their babies strapped to their backs. What need has he to practice farming?"

13.5

子曰:"诵《诗》三百,授之以政,不达[1];使于四方,不能专对[2],虽多,亦奚以为[3]?"

【中译文】

孔子说:"熟读《诗经》三百篇,派他处理政事,却不明白如何处理;派他作各国使臣,却不能独立地处理问题,读得再多,又有什么用呢?"

【注 释】

1 达:通达,通晓;会处理,会运用。

2 专对:即根据外交的具体情况,随机应变,独立行事,回答问题,办理交涉。外交使臣在处理对外交涉的事务时,因不可能时时事事都向本国朝廷请求指示,所以必须有"专对"的能力。又,当时在外交上往

论语意解

13.4

樊迟请学稼[1]。子曰:"吾不如老农。"请学为圃[2] 曰:"吾不如老圃。"

樊迟出。子曰:"小人哉,樊须也!上好礼,则民莫敢不敬;上好义,则民莫敢不服;上好信,则民莫敢不用情。夫如是,则四方之民襁负其子而至矣[3],焉用稼!"

【中译文】

樊迟请教如何种庄稼。孔子说:"我不如老农夫。"樊迟请教如何种菜。孔子说:"我不如老菜农。"樊迟出去了。孔子说:"真是小人呀,樊须。上边重视礼,百姓就不敢不尊敬;上边重视义,百姓就不敢不服从;上边讲求信用,百姓就不敢不讲真话。假如做到这样,四方的百姓就会背着小孩前来投奔,哪用得着自己去种庄稼呢?"

【注 释】

1 樊迟:姓樊,名须,字子迟。参阅《为政篇第二》第五章注。

2 圃(pǔ):菜地,菜园。引申为种菜。

3 襁(qiǎng):背婴儿的背带、布兜。

【英译文】

Fan Chi asked the Master to teach him about farming. The Master said, "You had better consult some old farmer." He asked about gardening. The Master said, "You had better ask some old vegetable-gardener."

When Fan Chi left, the Master said, "Fan is no gentleman! When those at the top love the rites, the people won't fail to be respectful; when justice is observed at the top, the people will be obedient; when sincerity reigns at the top, the people will be honest. Then, when such a situation prevails, people will flock to him from all sides with their babies strapped to their backs. What need has he to practice farming?"

13.5

子曰："诵《诗》三百，授之以政，不达；使于四方，不能专对；虽多，亦奚以为？"

【中译文】

孔子说："熟读《诗经》三百篇，派他去处理政事，却不明白如何处理；派他出各国使臣，却不能独立应对，诵得再多，又有什么用呢？"

【注释】

1 达：通达，通晓；会处理，会运用。

2 专对：即依据外交的具体情形，随机应变，独立行事，回答问题，办理交涉。外交使臣在执行任务交涉事务时，因不可能事事请示而国内事先指示，所以必须有"专对"的能力。又，"专对"在古代外交场合也指……

13.4

樊迟请学稼。子曰："吾不如老农。"请学为圃。曰："吾不如老圃。"樊迟出。子曰："小人哉！樊须也！上好礼，则民莫敢不敬；上好义，则民莫敢不服；上好信，则民莫敢不用情。夫如是，则四方之民襁负其子而至矣，焉用稼！"

【中译文】

樊迟请求孔子教他种庄稼。孔子说："我不如老农夫。"樊迟又请求学种菜。孔子说："我不如老菜农。"樊迟出去了。孔子说："真是小人啊，樊须！上边重视礼，百姓就没有不敬的；上边重视义，百姓就没有不服的；上边重视信，百姓就没有不讲真情的。做到像这样，四方的百姓就会背着小孩前来投奔，哪里用得着自己去种庄稼呢？"

【注释】

1 樊迟：姓樊，名须，字子迟，参阅《为政篇第二》第五章注。

2 圃(pǔ)：菜地，菜园。引申为种菜。

3 襁(qiǎng)：背婴儿的背带，布兜。

往以背诵《诗经》章句来委婉地进行提问和回答，故"诵诗三百"是外交人才的必备条件。

3 以：用。为：句末语助词，表示感慨或疑问。

【英译文】

The Master (Confucius) said, A man may be able to recite the three hundred poems in The Book of Poetry, however, when given a post in the government, he cannot turn his merits to account, or when sent on a mission to far parts he cannot answer particular questions, however extensive his knowledge may be, of what use is it to him?

13.6

子曰："其身正，不令而行；其身不正，虽令不从。"

【中译文】

孔子说："自身端正，不发命令，也会得到贯彻；自身不正，即使发布命令，也不会得到贯彻。"

【英译文】

The Master (Confucius) said, If the ruler himself is upright all will go well even though he does not give orders. But if he is not personally upright, even though he gives orders, they will not be obeyed.

13.7

子曰："鲁卫之政[1]，兄弟也。"

【中译文】

孔子说："鲁国、卫国的政治，如同兄弟一般相关联。"

【注释】

1 鲁卫之政：鲁国是周公（姬旦）的封地，卫国是周公的弟弟康叔　的封地。鲁、卫本兄弟之国，后来衰乱又相似，孔子遂有这样的　感叹。

【英译文】

The Master (Confucius) said, In their politics Lu state and Wei state are still brothers.

13.8

子谓卫公子荆善居室[1]。始有，曰："苟合矣[2]。"少有，曰："苟完矣。"富有，曰："苟美矣。"

【中译文】

孔子说卫国公子荆善于管理家业。刚有一些财产，公子荆便说："差不多够用了。"再增加一些财产时，他说："差不多足够了。"到财产富足时，说："差不多接

论语意解

13.7

子曰:"鲁卫之政,兄弟也。"

【中译文】

孔子说:"鲁国的政治,卫国的政治,如同兄弟一样相关。"

【注释】

1 鲁卫之政:鲁国是周公(旦)的封地,卫国是周公
的弟弟康叔的封地。当时,卫不况弱之国,治未宽缓
又相近似,故孔子有这样的一番议论。

【英译文】

The Master (Confucius) said, in their politics Lu state and Wei state are still brothers.

13.8

子谓卫公子荆善居室。始有,曰:"苟合
矣。"少有,曰:"苟完矣。"富有,曰:
"苟美矣。"

【中译文】

孔子评论卫国的公子荆善于管理家业。刚有一些财产,
公子荆便说:"差不多够用了。"有增加一些以后,他
说:"差不多完备了。"到拥有丰富的财产,说:"差不多完

13.7

子曰:"诵《诗》三百,授之以政,不达;使
于四方,不能专对;虽多,亦奚以为?"

故"而已矣"是"除诵文人么的必然条件。
3 以:用。达:此承语前而言,交涉谈判通畅。

【英译文】

The Master (Confucius) said, A man may be able to recite the three hundred poems in The Book of Poetry, however, when given a post in the government, he cannot turn his merits to account, or when sent on a mission to far parts he cannot answer particular questions, however extensive his knowledge may be, of what use is it to him?

13.6

子曰:"其身正,不令而行;其身不正,虽
令不从。"

【中译文】

孔子说:"自身端正,不发命令,也会得到贯彻执行;
自身不正,即使发布命令,也不会得到贯彻执行。"

【英译文】

The Master (Confucius) said, If the ruler himself is upright all will go well even though he does not give orders. But if he is not personally upright, even though he gives orders, they will not be obeyed.

呢？”孔子说：“让他们富裕起来。”冉有说：“已经富裕了，又该怎么办呢？”孔子说：“教育他们。”

【注释】

1 适：往，到，去。

2 仆：驾车。

3 庶（shù）：众多。这里指卫国人口众多。

4 何加：即“加何”。增加什么，进一步干什么、办什么。

5 教：教育，教化。孔子主张“先富而后教”。

【英译文】

When the Master (Confucius) was going to Wei state Ran You him. The Master said, What a large population! Ran You said, When the people have multiplied, what next should be done for them? The Master said, Enrich them. Ran You said, When one has enriched them, what next should be done for them? The Master said, Educate them.

13.10

子曰："苟有用我者[1]，期月而已可也[2]，三年有成。"

【中译文】

孔子说："如果有人用我治理国家，一年就会有起色了，三年就会大有成效。"

论语意解

近于完美了。"

【注释】

1 公子荆：卫国的大夫，字南楚。是卫献公的儿子，故称公子荆。传说他十五岁就代理宰相，处理国事。对自己的家业和生活享受，能随时知足，不奢侈。吴国的公子季札，曾把公子荆列为卫国的君子(见《左传·襄公二十九年》)。善居室：善于管理家业、管理财务经济，会过日子。

2 苟：差不多，也算是。

【英译文】

The Master (Confucius) said of Gong Zijing of the Wei State, He dwelt as a man should dwell in his house. When things began to prosper with him, he said, 'Now they will begin to be a little more suitable.' When he was better off still, he said, 'Now they will be fairly complete.' When he was really rich, he said, 'Now I shall be able to make them quite beautiful.'

13.9

子适卫[1]，冉有仆[2]。子曰："庶矣哉[3]！"冉有曰："既庶矣，又何加焉[4]？"曰："富之。"曰："既富矣，又何加焉？"曰："教之[5]。"

【中译文】

孔子到卫国去，冉有为他驾车。孔子说："卫国的人真多啊！"冉有说："人已经多了，接着该怎么办

13.9

【原文】

子适卫，冉有仆。子曰："庶矣哉！"冉有曰："既庶矣，又何加焉？"曰："富之。"曰："既富矣，又何加焉？"曰："教之。"

【译文】

The Master (Confucius) was going to Wei state. Ran You drove him. When the Master said, "How numerous are the people!" Ran You said, "When they have been made numerous, what more should be done for them?" The Master said, "Enrich them." Ran You said, "When they have been enriched, what more should be done for them?" The Master said, "Teach them."

【注释】

13.10

【原文】

子曰："苟有用我者，期月而已可也，三年有成。"

【译文】

The Master said, "If any prince were to employ me, in the course of twelve months, I should have done something considerable. In three years, the government would be perfected."

【注释】

13.12

子曰："如有王者[1]，必世而后仁[2]。"

【中译文】

孔子说："如果有王者兴起，必待三十年以后才能实现仁政。"

【注释】

1 王者：能治国安邦、以德行仁的贤明君主。
2 世：三十年是一世。

【英译文】

The Master (Confucius) said, If a Kingly Man were to arise, within a single generation Goodness would prevail.

13.13

子曰："苟正其身矣，于从政乎何有？不能正其身，如正人何？"

【中译文】

孔子说："如果自身端正，从事政治还有什么困难呢？自身不能端正，怎样使别人端正呢？"

【英译文】

The Master (Confucius) said, Once a man has contrived to put himself

【注释】

1 苟：如果，假如。
2 期月：周一年十二个月，即一周年。"期(jī)，周。

【英译文】

The Master (Confucius) said, If only someone were to employ me, even for a single year, I could do a great deal; and in three years I could finish off the whole work.

13.11

子曰："'善人为邦百年，亦可以胜残去杀矣。'诚哉是言也[1]！"

【中译文】

孔子说："'善人治理国家一百年，也就可以教化残暴、免去刑杀了。' 真对啊，这话！"

【注释】

1 是：代词。这，此。

【英译文】

The Master (Confucius) said, 'If a good man had charge of a country for a hundred years it would become really possible to stop cruelty and do away with slaughter.' How true the saying is!

13.15

定公问："一言而可以兴邦，有诸[1]？"

孔子对曰："言不可以若是，其几也[2]，人之言曰：'为君难，为臣不易。'如知为君之难也，不几乎一言而兴邦乎？"

曰："一言而丧邦，有诸？"

孔子对曰："言不可以若是，其几也，人之言曰：'予无乐乎为君，唯其言而莫予违也。'如其善而莫之违也，不亦善乎？如不善而莫之违也，不几乎一言而丧邦乎？"

【中译文】

鲁定公问："一句话就可以振兴国家，有这样的事吗？"孔子回答说："话不可以讲得像这样肯定，但有与这接近的，有人说：'做君主难，做臣也不容易。'如果知道做君主难，这岂不接近于'一句话就可以使国家振兴'吗？"鲁定公说："一句话就可以使国家灭亡，有这样的话吗？"孔子回答说："话不可以讲得像这样肯定，但有与这接近的，有人说：'我做君主并没有什么可高兴的，只是高兴我说的话没有人违抗。'如果君主说的话正确，而没有人违抗，不也是很好吗？如果说的话不正确，而没有人违抗，这岂不接近于'一句话就可以使国家灭亡'吗？"

aright, he will find no difficulty at all in filling any government post. But if he cannot put himself aright, how can he correct others?

13.14

冉子退朝[1]。子曰："何晏也[2]？"对曰："有政。"子曰："其事也。如有政，虽不吾以[3]，吾其与闻之。"

【中译文】

冉求从季氏官府办完公事回来。孔子说："为何回来晚了？"冉求回答说："有政务。"孔子说："是季氏的私事吧。如果是国家政务，虽然我参与不了，我也会有所耳闻的。"

【注释】

1 冉子：冉求。曾任季氏宰（家臣）。参阅《八佾篇第三》第六章注。

2 晏（yàn）：晚，迟。

3 吾以：用我。"以"，用。

【英译文】

Once when Master Ran You came back from Court, the Master said, Why are you so late? He replied, There were affairs of State. The Master said, You must mean private business. If there had been affairs of State, although I have no official post, I too should have been bound to hear of them.

13.15

【原文】

定公问："一言而可以兴邦，有诸？"
孔子对曰："言不可以若是，其几也。人之言曰：'为君难，为臣不易。'如知为君之难也，不几乎一言而兴邦乎？"
曰："一言而丧邦，有诸？"
孔子对曰："言不可以若是，其几也。人之言曰：'予无乐乎为君，唯其言而莫予违也。'如其善而莫之违也，不亦善乎？如不善而莫之违也，不几乎一言而丧邦乎？"

【中译文】

鲁定公问："一句话就可以使国家兴盛，有这样的事吗？"孔子回答说："话不可以这样简单地讲效果。但是人们说：'做君难，做臣不容易。'如果知道做君难，这岂不接近于一句话就可以使国家兴盛吗？"鲁定公又说："一句话就可以使国家衰败，有这样的事吗？"孔子回答说："话不可以这样简单地讲效果。不过人们说：'我做国君并没有别的快乐，只是我说什么话都没有人敢违抗。'如果说得对而没有人违抗，不也很好吗？如果说得不对而没有人违抗，这岂不接近于一句话就可以使国家衰败吗？"

---

might, he will find no difficulty at all in filling any government post. But if he cannot put himself aright, how can he correct others?

13.14

【原文】

冉子退朝。子曰："何晏也？"对曰："有政。"子曰："其事也。如有政，虽不吾以，吾其与闻之。"

【中译文】

冉有从朝廷回来。孔子说："为什么回来得这么晚呀？"冉有回答说："有政事。"孔子说："那只是一般的事务罢了。如果是国家政事，虽然我现在不做官了，我也会知道它的。"

【注释】

1. 退朝：由朝廷退下来，指办完公事。
2. 晏(yàn)：晚。
3. 吾以：用我，"以"，用。

【英译文】

Once when Master Jan You came back from Court, the Master said, Why are you so late? He replied, There were affairs of State. The Master said, You must mean private business. If there had been affairs of State, although I have no official post, I too should have been bound to hear of them.

【注释】

1 诸："之乎"二字的合音。

2 几(jī)：将近，接近。

【英译文】

Duke Ding of the Lu State asked if there was one word the state could be made prosperous by.

The Master (Confucius) replied, "There is no such word. But there is one that comes near it. There is a saying: 'It is hard to be a prince and not easy to be a minister.' If the subjects really understood the difficulties of being a prince, they would all work hard. Is it possible that the state can be made prosperous by one word?"

Duke Ding asked if there was one word that could ruin a state.

The Master (Confucius) replied, "There is no such word. But there is one that comes near it. There is a saying: 'What pleasure is there in being a prince, unless one can say whatever one chooses, and no one dares to disagree?' Isn't that a good thing if what he says is correct and no one opposes it? But if what he says is incorrect and no one opposes it, would not the state be ruined by one word?"

13.16

叶公问政¹。子曰："近者说，远者来。"

【中译文】

叶公问怎样从政。孔子说："使自己境内的百姓生活快乐，别国的百姓来投靠依附。"

【注 释】

1 叶公：姓沈，名诸梁，楚国大夫。参阅《述而篇第七》第十九章注。

【英译文】

Duke she asked about government. The Master said, when the near approve and the distant approach.

13.17

子夏为莒父宰¹，问政。子曰："无欲速，无见小利。欲速则不达，见小利则大事不成。"

【中译文】

子夏到莒父当地方长官，问怎样为政。孔子说："不要企求速成，不要贪图小利。企求速成，往往达不到目的；贪图小利，往往做不成大事。"

【注 释】

1 莒父(jǔ fǔ)：鲁国城邑名，在今山东省莒县境内。一说，在高密县东南。

【英译文】

When Zi Xia was governor of Jufu Country, he asked for advice about government. The Master said, Do not try to hurry things. Ignore minor considerations. If you hurry things, your personality will not come into play. If you let yourself be distracted by minor considerations, nothing important will

论语意解

【注释】
1. 庶："之乎"二字的合音。
2. 汜（sì）：水名，接纥。

【英译文】

Duke Ding of the Lu State asked if there was one word the state could be made prosperous by.

The Master (Confucius) replied, "There is no such word. But there is one that comes near it. There is a saying: It is hard to be a prince and not easy to be a minister. If the subjects really understood the difficulties of being a prince, they would all work hard. Is it possible that the state can be made prosperous by one word?"

Duke Ding asked if there was one word that could ruin a state.

The Master (Confucius) replied, "There is no such word. But there is one that comes near it. There is a saying. What pleasure is there in being a prince, unless one can say whatever one chooses, and no one dares to disagree? Isn't that a good thing if what he says is correct and no one opposes it? But if what he says is incorrect and no one opposes it, would it not the state be ruined by one word?"

13.16

叶公问政。子曰："近者说，远者来。"

【中译文】

叶公向孔子请教为政之道，孔子说："要使自己境内的百姓高兴满意，别国的百姓也来投奔你。"

【注释】

1. 叶公：姓沈，名诸梁，字子高（参见前篇第七章第十六章注）。

【英译文】

Duke she asked about government. The Master said, when the near approve and the distant approach.

13.17

子夏为莒父宰，问政。子曰："无欲速，无见小利。欲速则不达，见小利则大事不成。"

【中译文】

子夏当了莒父邑的总管，向孔子请教为政之道，孔子说："不要急于求成，不要贪图小利。急于求成，往往欲速则不达；贪图小利，常常使得大事不成。"

【注释】

1. 莒父（jǔ fǔ）：当时鲁国城邑，在今山东省莒县境内。

【英译文】

When Zi Xia was governor of Jufu County, he asked for advice about government. The Master said, Do not try to hurry things. Ignore minor considerations. If you hurry things, your personality will not come into play. If you let yourself be distracted by minor considerations, nothing important will sort of uprightness.

13.19

樊迟问仁。子曰："居处恭，执事敬，与人忠。虽之夷狄[1]，不可弃也。"

【中译文】

樊迟问怎样是仁。孔子说："在家能恭敬规矩，办事能认真谨慎，对人能忠实诚恳。虽然到了夷狄，也不会遭受遗弃。"

【注释】

1 之：动词。到，去，往。

【英译文】

Fan Chi asked about Goodness. The Master said, In daily life, courteous, in public life, diligent, in relationships, loyal. This is a maxim that no matter where you may be, even amid the barbarians of the east or north, may never be set aside.

13.20

子贡问曰："何如斯可谓之士矣？"子曰："行己有耻，使于四方，不辱君命，可谓士矣。"

曰："敢问其次？"

论语意解

三三二 三三一

---

ever get finished.

13.18

叶公语孔子曰："吾党有直躬者[1]，其父攘羊而子证之[2]。"孔子曰："吾党之直者异于是，父为子隐[3]，子为父隐，直在其中矣。"

【中译文】

叶公对孔子说："我的老家有个正直的人，他父亲偷了羊，他去告发。"孔子说："我们家乡的正直的人和你所讲的不一样：父亲为儿子隐瞒，儿子为父亲隐瞒，正直的品德就在其中了。"

【注释】

1 直躬者：犹言正直、坦率的人。"躬"，身。
2 攘（rǎng）：偷，窃，抢。证：检举，告发。
3 父为子隐："隐"，隐瞒，隐讳。儒家提倡父慈子孝，即使对方有错，也要在外人面前为之隐瞒，以全父子之恩、父子之情。儒家认为，保住亲情之恩义，是其他社会行为的基础。

【英译文】

Duke she said to the Master, In my country there was a man called Upright Kung. His father appropriated a sheep, and Kung bore witness against him. Master Kung said, In my country the upright men are of quite another sort. A father will screen his son, and a son his father-which incidentally does involve a

13.18

叶公语孔子曰:"吾党有直躬者，其父攘羊，而子证之。"孔子曰:"吾党之直者异于是，父为子隐，子为父隐，直在其中矣。"

【中译文】

叶公对孔子说:"我的家乡有个正直的人，他父亲偷了羊，他去告发。"孔子说:"我们家乡的正直的人和你所讲的不一样：父亲为儿子隐瞒，儿子为父亲隐瞒，正直的品德就在其中了。"

【注释】

1 直躬者：能言正直、做事公正的人。"躬"，身。
2 攘(rǎng)：偷，窃。私，此指偷窃。
3 父为子隐："隐"，隐瞒，隐讳。儒家提倡父慈子孝，即使对方有错，也要替对方加以隐瞒，以全父子之爱。父子之间情，隐瞒其为，便其成为立身之基础。

【英译文】

Duke she said to the Master, In my country, there was a man called Upright Kung. His father appropriated a sheep, and Kung bore witness against him. Master Kung said, In my country the upright men are of quite another sort. A father will screen his son, and a son his father — which incidentally does involve a sort of uprightness.

13.19

樊迟问仁。子曰:"居处恭，执事敬，与人忠。虽之夷狄，不可弃也。"

【中译文】

樊迟向孔子请教关于仁的问题。孔子说:"平常在家规规矩矩，办入事要谨慎，待人忠诚老实。即使到了夷狄，也不会背弃这些。"

【注释】

1 之：动词，到，去，往。

【英译文】

Fan Ch'ih asked about Goodness. The Master said, In daily life, courteous, in public life, diligent, in relationships, loyal. This is a maxim that no matter where you may be, even amid the barbarians of the east or north may never be set aside.

13.20

子贡问曰:"何如斯可谓之士矣?"子曰:"行己有耻，使于四方，不辱君命，可谓士矣。"

曰:"敢问其次?"

曰："宗族称孝焉，乡党称弟焉¹。"

曰："敢问其次？"

曰："言必信，行必果。硁硁然小人哉²，抑亦可以为次矣。"

曰："今之从政者何如？"子曰："噫！斗筲之人³，何足算也！"

【中译文】

子贡问："怎样做才配称为知识分子？"孔子说："对自己的行为能保持羞耻之心；出使到其他国家，能不辜负君主的使命，这样的人可配称为知识分子了。"子贡说："斗胆问，次一等的呢？"孔子说："宗族里的人称赞他孝顺父母，乡里的人称赞他敬爱兄长。"子贡说："斗胆问，再次一等的呢？"孔子说："说话一定守信用，行动一定坚决果断。这样是浅薄固执的小老百姓，不过也可以作为次一等的了。"子贡说："如今从政的人如何呢？"孔子说："咳！这些器量狭小的人怎么值得一提啊？"

【注释】

1 弟：同"悌"。敬爱兄长。

2 硁硁然："硁（kēng）"，通"铿"，小石坚确貌。形容浅薄固执。孔子认为如果不问是非曲直，在大事上糊涂，只管自己的言行"必信""必果"，必

然会陷于浅薄固执。《孟子·离娄下》说："大人者，言不必信，行不必果，惟义所在。"意思是：真正有德行的人，说话不一定句句守信，行为不一定贯彻始终，只要合乎道义，按道义行事便成。这话可作为《论语》本章的补充。

3 斗筲："筲（shāo）"，盛饭用的小竹器，饭筐。斗、筲容量都不大（一斗只容十升；一筲只容五升，一说容一斗二升），引申来形容人的见识短浅，器量狭小。

【英译文】

Zi Gong asked, "What must a man be like to merit the title of a gentleman?" The Master (Confucius) said, "The man who has a sense of shame in his personal conduct and does not disgrace his prince's commission as an envoy to distant lands—such a man may be called a gentleman." Zi Gong said, "May I venture to ask who would rank next?" The Master said, "The man who is known in his clan for filial duty, and in his village for fraternal duty."

13.21

子曰："不得中行而与之¹，必也狂狷乎²！狂者进取，狷者有所不为也。"

【中译文】

孔子说："得不到行中庸之道的人为友，那一定要同狂者和狷者交往了。狂者有进取心，敢作敢为；狷

【英译文】

Zi Gong asked, "What must a man be like to merit the title of a gentleman?" The Master (Confucius) said, "The man who has a sense of shame in his personal conduct and does not disgrace his prince's commission as an envoy to distant lands-such a man may be called a gentleman." Zi Gong said, "May I venture to ask who would rank next?" The Master said, "The man who is known in his clan for filial duty, and in his village for fraternal duty"

13.21

子曰:"不得中行而与之,必也狂狷乎!狂者进取,狷者有所不为也。"

【注释】

1 巫医:"巫",巫师,能降神占卜的人。"医",医师。古代巫、医往往合于一身,巫师亦往往掌握一定的医术,或以禳祷之术替人疗疾。朱熹说:"巫,所以交鬼神;医,所以寄死生。故虽贱役,而犹不可以无常。"

2 "不恒"二句:见《易经·恒卦·九三爻辞》。意为:做人如果不能永恒地保持自己的德行(三心二意,没有操守),免不了要承受招来的羞辱。

3 占:占卜,算卦。孔子这句话的言下之意或为:没有恒心的人一定遇凶,用不着再去占卜了。

【英译文】

The Master (Confucius) said, "The men from the south have a saying which goes, 'If a man lacks constancy, he will not even make a witch-doctor.' Well said! The Book of changes says, 'If a man lacks constancy in virtue and morality, he may incur disgrace.' " The Master went on to say, "Failure to strive for constancy simply means that one will not necessarily use the book of divination."

13.23

子曰:"君子和而不同[1],小人同而不和。"

【中译文】

孔子说:"君子主张和谐共处而不强求一致;小人

论语意解

三三六 三三五

者拘谨,洁身自好,有所不为。"

【注释】

1 中行:合乎中庸之道的言行。与:相与,交往,来往;向他传道,同他共事。

2 狂:指志意高远,纵情任性,骄傲自大,但勇往直前,敢作敢为,有进取精神。狷(juàn):指为人耿直拘谨,洁身自好,安分守己,不求有所作为亦绝不肯同流合污。

【英译文】

The Master (Confucius) said, "If I can't find moderate men to associate with, I must turn to the impetuous or the upright. The former will always progress and the latter will not do bad things."

13.22

子曰:"南人有言曰:'人而无恒,不可以作巫医[1]。'善夫!'不恒其德,或承之羞[2]。'"子曰:"不占而已矣[3]。"

【中译文】

孔子说:"南方人有句话说:'人如果没有恒心,就不可以作巫医。'这话真好啊!《易经》上也说:'如果不能永恒地保持自己的德行,免不了要承受羞辱。'"孔子又说:"俗:'吾一语点破,不用占卦了。"

论语通解

【注释】

1 巫医："巫"、"医"。指替神占卜的人。"医"，医治。古代巫、医往往合而为一，既以巫术亦以医道，后来的医术，则以医病为本替人治病。未尝说："巫，能以交鬼事。医，则以治病也。故连称之。"而巫、医可以无常。

2 "不恒"二句：见《易经·恒卦·九三爻辞》。意为：做人如果不能永远地保持自己的德行（三心二意，变有异心），免不了要承受得来的羞辱。

3 占：占卜。孔子这句话的意思是：没有恒心的人，一定遭遇凶，用不着再去占卜了。

【英译文】

The Master (Confucius) said, "The men from the south have a saying which goes, 'If a man lacks constancy, he will not even make a witch-doctor.' Well said! The Book of changes says, 'If a man lacks constancy in virtue and morality, he may incur disgrace.'" The Master went on to say, "Failure to strive for constancy simply means that one will not necessarily use the book of divination."

13.23

子曰："君子和而不同，小人同而不和。"

【中译文】

孔子说："君子讲求和谐而协调共处而不苟同附和，小人...

【注释】

1 中行：合乎中庸之道的言行。行：相反。父狂、狷：向他传道，向他共道。

2 狂：满志意高远，勇往任性。狷（juàn）：拘谨自守。有进取精神。狷（juàn）：拘谨自守。安分守己，不求人知狂狷于非道，未有必须持进退做不肯同流合污。

【英译文】

The Master (Confucius) said, "If I can't find moderate men to associate with, I must turn to the impetuous or the upright. The former will always progress and the latter will not do bad things."

13.22

子曰："南人有言曰：'人而无恒，不可以作巫医。'善夫!'不恒其德，或承之羞。'"子曰："不占而已矣。"

【中译文】

孔子说："南方人有句话说：'人如果没有恒心，就不可以作巫医。'这句真好啊!《易经》上也说：'如果不能永远保持自己的德行，免不了要承受羞辱。'"孔子说："答一句话：不用去占卜了。"

"未必真好。"子贡又问："乡人都憎恶的人，如何呢？"
孔子说："未必真坏。比不上那些乡人中的好人都喜欢
他，坏人都讨厌他的人。"

【英译文】

Zi Gong asked, saying, What would you feel about a man who was loved by all his fellow-villagers? The Master said, That is not enough. Zi Gong asked again, What would you feel about a man who was hated by all his fellow-villagers? The Master said, That is not enough. Best of all would be that the good people in his village loved him and the bad hated him.

13.25

子曰："君子易事而难说也[1]。说之不以道，不说也。及其使人也，器之。小人难事而易说也。说之虽不以道，说也。及其使人也，求备焉。"

【中译文】

孔子说："为君子做事容易，讨他喜欢却很难。不以正道去讨他的喜欢，他是不高兴的。而到他使用人的时候，能按才能的大小合理使用他。给小人做事很困难，讨他喜欢却容易。虽然不以正道去讨他的喜欢，他也会喜欢的。而到他使用人的时候，对人就求全责备。"

论语意解

三三八　三三七

强求一致而不能和谐共处。"

【注释】

1 和，同：这是春秋时代常用的两个概念。"和"，和谐，调和，互相协调。指不同性质的各种因素的和谐统一。如五味的调和，八音的合谐。君子尚义，无乖戾之心，能和谐共处，但不盲从附和，能用自己的正确意见来纠正别人的错误意见，故说"和而不同"。"同"，相同，同类，同一。小人尚利，在利益一致时，互相阿比，同流合污，能够"同"；然一旦利益发生冲突，则不能和谐共处，更不能用道义来协调人情世故。故说"同而不和"。

【英译文】

The Master (Confucius) said, The true gentleman is conciliatory but not accommodating. A petty man is accommodating but not conciliatory.

13.24

子贡问曰："乡人皆好之，何如？"子曰："未可也。""乡人皆恶之，何如？"子曰："未可也，不如乡人之善者好之，其不善者恶之。"

【中译文】

子贡问："乡人都喜欢的人，如何呢？"孔子说：

子曰："君子和而不同，小人同而不和。"

【英译文】

The Master (Confucius) said, "The true gentleman is conciliatory but not accommodating. A petty man is accommodating but not conciliatory."

13.24

子贡问曰："乡人皆好之，何如？"子曰："未可也。""乡人皆恶之，何如？"子曰："未可也。不如乡人之善者好之，其不善者恶之。"

【中译文】

子贡问："乡人都喜欢的人，怎么样？"孔子说："未可也。""乡人都厌恶的人，怎么样？"孔子说："未可也。不如乡里的好人都喜欢他，坏人都厌恶他。"

【英译文】

Zi Gong asked, saying, What would you feel about a man who was loved by all his fellow-villagers? The Master said, That is not enough. Zi Gong asked again, What would you feel about a man who was hated by all his fellow-villagers? The Master said, That is not enough. Best of all would be that the good people in his village loved him and the bad hated him.

13.25

子曰："君子易事而难说也：说之不以道，不说也；及其使人也，器之。小人难事而易说也：说之虽不以道，说也；及其使人也，求备焉。"

【中译文】

孔子说："为君子干事容易，讨他的喜欢却很难：不以正当手段讨他的喜欢，他是不高兴的；而到他使用人的时候，总能量才器使。给小人做事很困难，讨他的喜欢却容易：虽然不以正当手段讨他的喜欢，他也会喜欢的；而到他使用人的时候，对人总求全责备。"

【注释】

1 和、同：这是春秋时代常用的两个概念。"和"，和谐、调和、正相协调，指不同性质的各种因素的和谐统一，调五味的调和，八音的合奏，都不尚义。无所违乎心，能和而谐其异，能和而不同。"同"，和同，同类。小人尚和，在和益。致出如相同比，阿流合污。但是，"同"，然一旦利益发生冲突，则不能和谐共处，更不能用道又来协调而彼此相攻故曰，"同而不和。"

【英译文】

The Master (Confucius) said, A gentleman is dignified, but never haughty; A petty man is haughty, but never dignified.

13.27

子曰："刚，毅，木[1]，讷[2]，近仁。"

【中译文】

孔子说："刚强，坚毅，朴实，寡言，这四种品德接近于仁。"

【注释】

1 木：质朴，朴实，憨厚老实。

2 讷：说话迟钝。引申为言语非常谨慎，不肯轻易说话。

【英译文】

The Master (Confucius) said, Imperturbable, resolute, tree-like, slow to speak-such a one is near to Goodness.

13.28

子路问曰："何如斯可谓之士矣？"子曰："切切偲偲[1]，怡怡如也[2]，可谓士矣。朋友切切偲偲，兄弟怡怡。"

论语意解

三四〇 三三九

【注释】

1 易事：易与共事，事奉他、给他做事容易。说：同"悦"。

【英译文】

The Master (Confucius) said, The True gentleman is easy to serve, yet difficult to please. For if you try to please him in any manner inconsistent with the Way, he refuses to be pleased; but in using the services of others he only expects of them what they are capable of performing. A petty man difficult to serve, but easy to please. Even though you try to please them in a manner inconsistent with the Way, they will still be pleased; but in using the services of others they expect them (irrespective of their capacities) to do any work that comes along.

13.26

子曰："君子泰而不骄[1]、小人骄而不泰。"

【中译文】

孔子说："君子内心沉静而不骄傲狂躁，小人骄傲狂躁而内心不沉静。"

【注释】

1 泰，骄：皇侃《论语义疏》："君子坦荡荡，心貌怡平，是泰而不为骄慢也；小人性好轻凌，而心恒戚戚，是骄而不泰也。"朱熹说："君子循理，故安舒而不矜肆。小人逞欲，故反是。"

【英译文】

The Master (Confucius) said, Only when men of the right sort have instructed a people for seven years ought there to be any talk of engaging them in warfare.

13.30

子曰："以不教民战[1]，是谓弃之。"

【中译文】

孔子说："让没有经过军事训练的人去打仗，这就是抛弃他们。"

【注释】

1 不教民：即"不教之民"。没有经过军事教育训练的人。

【英译文】

The Master (Confucius) said, To lead into battle a people that has not first been instructed is to betray them.

论语意解

三四二　三四一

【中译文】

子路问："如何才配称为'士'呢？"孔子说："互相勉励督促，待人亲切和气，就可以称为'士'了。朋友之间要互相勉励督促，兄弟之间要和睦相处。"

【注释】

1 切切偲偲(sī)：恳切地责勉、告诫，善意地互相批评；相互切磋，相互督促，和睦相处。
2 怡怡(yí)：和气，安适，愉快。

【英译文】

Zi Lu asked, What must a man be like, that he may be called a true knight of the Way? The Master said, He must be critical and exacting, but at the same time indulgent. Then he may be called a true knight. Critical and exacting with regard to the conduct of his friends; indulgent towards his brothers.

13.29

子曰："善人教民七年[1]，亦可以即戎矣[2]。"

【中译文】

孔子说："有作为的领导人教导百姓七年，就可以使百姓备战为国了。"

【注释】

1 善人：好的有作为的领导人。一说，善于治军作战的人。
2 即：靠近，从事，参加。戎(róng)：军队，战争。

【中译文】

子路问："如何不能称为'士'呢？"孔子说："相互勉励督促，彼此和睦相处，这才可以称为'士'。对朋友间要相互勉励督促，兄弟之间要和睦相处。"

【注释】

1 切切偲偲(sī)：恳切劝勉貌。切切，恳切貌，常察地互相批评；偲偲，相互勉励，相互督促，和睦相处。

2 怡怡(yí)：和气、亲近、愉快。

【英译文】

Zi Lu asked, What must a man be like, that he may be called a true knight of the Way? The Master said, He must be critical and exacting, but at the same time indulgent. Then he may be called a true knight. Critical and exacting with regard to the conduct of his friends; indulgent towards his brothers.

13.29

子曰："善人教民七年，亦可以即戎矣。"

【中译文】

孔子说："有作为的善人教导老百姓七年，就可以使百姓准备去打仗了。"

【注释】

1 善人：近明行作为的贤导人。一说，善于指导无关无战的人。

2 即：靠近。从事，参加。戎(róng)：干戈，指战事。

13.30

子曰："以不教民战，是谓弃之。"

【中译文】

孔子说："让没有经过军事训练的人去打仗，这就是抛弃他们。"

【注释】

1 不教民：即"不教之民"。没有经过军事训练的人民。

【英译文】

The Master (Confucius) said, To lead into battle a people that has not first been instructed is to betray them.

【英译文】

The Master (Confucius) said, Only when men of the right sort have instructed a people for seven years ought there to be any talk of engaging them in warfare.

宪问篇第十四（共四十四章）

Confucius And His Students Talking about the Way of Being a Gentleman

14.1

宪问耻[1]。子曰："邦有道，谷[2]。邦无道，谷，耻也。"

"克、伐、怨、欲[3]，不行焉，可以为仁矣？"子曰："可以为难矣，仁则吾不知也。"

【中译文】

原宪问什么是可耻。孔子说："国家治政清明，可以做官拿俸禄。国家治政昏乱，仍然做官拿俸禄，就是可耻。"原宪又问："好胜，自夸，怨恨，贪婪，这些毛病都能克制，可以算做到了仁吧？"孔子说："可以说是很难做到，至于是否算仁，我不知道。"

【注释】

1 宪：即原思。参阅《雍也篇第六》第五章注。原思，当属于前章孔子所说的"狷者"类型的人物，故孔子言"邦有道"应有为而立功食禄，"邦无道"才应独善而不贪位慕禄，以激励原思的志向，使他自勉而进于有为。

2 谷：谷米。指当官拿俸禄。

3 克：争强好胜。伐：自我夸耀。怨：怨恨，恼怒。

论语意解

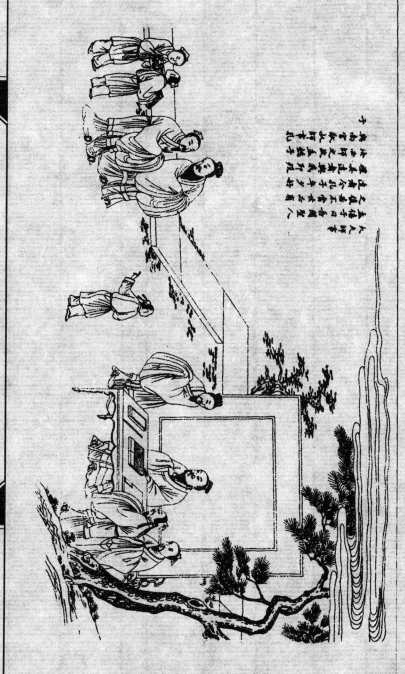

Senior Official Entrusting His sons to Confucius

宪问篇第十四 （共四十四章）

Confucius And His Students Talking about the Way of Being a Gentleman

14.1

宪问耻[1]。子曰："邦有道，谷[2]；邦无道，谷，耻也。"

"克、伐、怨、欲[3]不行焉，可以为仁矣？"子曰："可以为难矣，仁则吾不知也。"

【中译文】

原宪问什么是可耻。孔子说："国家政治清明，可以做官拿俸禄。国家政治败坏，仍然做官拿俸禄，这是可耻。"原宪又问："好胜、自夸、怨恨、贪婪，这些毛病都能克制，可以算做到了仁吗？"孔子说："可以说是很难做到，至于是否算仁，我不知道。"

【注释】

1. 宪：即原思。参阅《雍也篇第六》第五章注。原思当是孔子前章孔子所说的"隐者"类型的人物，故孔子于言"邦有道"，故有为而立而必身修善而不资位禄禄，以德绳隐思的志向，使他自励而进于有为。

2. 谷：谷米。指当官拿俸禄。

3. 克：争强好胜。伐：自我夸耀。怨：怨恨。欲：贪欲。

14.3

子曰："邦有道，危言危行[1]；邦无道，危行言孙[2]。"

【中译文】

孔子说："国家政治清明，要说话正直，行为正直；国家政治昏乱，行为仍要正直，但说话要谨慎。"

【注释】

1 危：正直。言人所不敢言，行人所不敢行。

2 孙：同"逊"。谦逊，恭顺。在这里，有随和顺从而谨慎之意。孔子认为，处乱世，要"言孙"以避祸，不应"危言"而招祸（作无谓牺牲）。

【英译文】

The Master (Confucius) said, When the Way prevails in the land, be bold in speech and bold in action. When the Way does not prevail, be bold in action but conciliatory in speech.

14.4

子曰："有德者必有言，有言者不必有德。仁者必有勇，勇者不必有仁。

【中译文】

孔子说："有德行的人一定有好的言论，有好的言

欲：贪求多欲。

【英译文】

Yuan Xian asked about shame. The Master said, "When a state is ruled according to the right way, a gentleman accepts rewards. But when a state is not ruled according to the right way, one is shameful if he accepts rewards." Yuan Xian asked again, "If a man does not insist on always being a winner, and if he is not given to boasting, resentment and greediness, may he be considered a gentleman?" The Master said, "He may be said to have done what is difficult; but I don't know whether he should be called a gentleman."

14.2

子曰："士而怀居[1]，不足以为士矣。

【中译文】

孔子说："作为知识分子，如果留恋家庭与田亩，就不足以成为知识分子。"

【注释】

1 怀居："怀"，留恋，思念。"居"，家居，家庭。《左传》上有"怀与安，实败名"的话（《僖公二十三年》），士若怀恋家居之安，心有所累，就成功不了事业。

【英译文】

The Master (Confucius) said, "The man who prefers his own ease and comfort is no gentleman at all."

论语意解

禄：贪求名利。

【英译文】
Yuan Xian asked about shame. The Master said, "When a state is ruled according to the right way, a gentleman accepts rewards. But when a state is not ruled according to the right way, one is shameful if he accepts rewards." Yuan Xian asked again, "If a man does not insist on always being a winner, and if he is not given to boasting, resentment and greediness, may he be considered a gentleman?" The Master said, "He may be said to have done what is difficult, but I don't know whether he should be called a gentleman."

14.2

子曰：“士而怀居，不足以为士矣。”

【中译文】
孔子说：“作为知识分子，如果留恋家室安乐的田地，就不足以成为知识分子。”

【注释】
1 怀居："怀"，留恋，思念。"居"，家居，家室。据《左传》上有"怀与安实，实败名"，即出《僖公二十三年》，士若怀恋家室之安，心有所顾累，就放弃不了事业。

【英译文】
The Master (Confucius) said, "The man who prefers his own ease and comfort is no gentleman at all."

14.3

子曰：“邦有道，危言危行；邦无道，危行言孙。”

【中译文】
孔子说：“国家政治清明，要正直地说正直地做；国家政治黑暗，行为依旧是正直，而说话要谨慎。”

【注释】
1 危：正直。当人那不敢言，行人那不敢行。
2 孙：同"逊"，谦逊，恭顺。在乱世，孔子认为，处乱世，避祸，不应"危言"，而揖稿（作无谓晒辞）。

【英译文】
The Master (Confucius) said, When the Way prevails in the land, be bold in speech and bold in action. When the Way does not prevail, be bold in action but conciliatory in speech.

14.4

子曰：“有德者必有言，有言者不必有德。仁者必有勇，勇者不必有仁。”

【中译文】
孔子说：“有德行的人一定有好听的言论，有好的言英雄。一是唐尧时的射箭能手。传说尧时十日并出，晒得大地河干草枯，羿射掉九日以解救民困。二是帝喾时的射师。三是夏时有穷国的君主。传说他本是夷族的一个酋长，曾一度篡夺了夏的政权而代理夏政。其理政后荒淫喜猎，把朝政交给亲信家臣寒浞（zhuó）管理。寒浞觊觎羿的地位和他美貌的妻子，收买了羿的家奴逄蒙，乘羿打猎回来毫无防备，将其杀害。本章中的羿即指有穷国的羿。

3 奡荡舟："奡（ào）"，一作"浇"。寒浞的儿子。是个大力士，又善于水战。传说他能"陆地行舟（在陆地上推着船走）"。"荡舟"，摇船，划船。据顾炎武《日知录》说：古人以左右冲杀为"荡"。这里便可理解为水战，即以舟师冲杀。《竹书纪年》曾记："奡伐斟寻，大战于淮，覆其舟，灭之。"后在征战中，奡被夏朝中兴之主少康所杀。

4 禹：夏代开国祖先，善治水，重视发展农业。稷（jì）：传说是帝喾之子，名弃，善农耕，尧举为农师。至舜时，受封于邰（今陕西省武功县西南），号曰"后稷"，别姓姬氏，是周朝的祖先。后世又被奉为谷神。

【英译文】

Nang gong Kuo asked the Master, saying, Yi was a mighty archer and Ao shook the boat; yet both of them came to a bad end. Whereas Yu and Ji, who devoted themselves to agriculture, came into possession of all that is under Heaven.

论语意解

三四八　三四七

论的人却不一定有德行。有仁义的人必定勇敢，勇敢的人却不一定有仁德。"

【英译文】

The Master (Confucius) said, The man who has accumulated moral power will certainly also possess eloquence; but he who has eloquence does not necessarily possess moral power. A Good Man will certainly also possess courage; but a brave man is not necessarily Good.

14.5

南宫适问于孔子曰[1]："羿善射[2]，奡荡舟[3]，俱不得其死然。禹、稷躬稼而有天下[4]。"夫子不答。南宫适出。子曰："君子哉若人！尚德哉若人！"

【中译文】

南宫适问孔子："羿善于射箭，奡善于水战，都不得好死。禹、稷亲自种庄稼，却取得了天下。"孔子没回答。南宫适出去了。孔子说："真是君子啊，这个人！真是尊崇仁德啊，这个人！"

【注释】

1 南宫适：孔子弟子。参阅《公冶长篇第五》第二章注。

2 羿：在上古神话传说中有三个羿，都是善于射箭的

【注释】

1 劳：勤劳，劳苦，操劳。此有进行劳动教育的含义。朱熹《四书集注》说："爱而知劳之，则其为爱也深矣；忠而知诲之，则其为忠也大矣。"《国语·鲁语下》："夫民劳则思，思则善心生；逸则淫，淫则忘善， 忘善则恶心生。"

【英译文】

The Master (Confucius) said, How can he be said truly to love, who exacts no effort from the objects of his love? How can he be said to be truly loyal, who refrains from admonishing the object of his loyalty?

14.8

子曰："为命¹，裨谌草创之²，世叔讨论之³，行人子羽修饰之⁴，东里子产润色之⁵。"

【中译文】

孔子说："郑国制定法令，总是由裨谌写出草稿；由世叔组织讨论；由外交官员子羽加以修饰；最后由东里的子产润色完成。"

【注释】

1 命：旧注谓指诸侯"盟会之辞"，即外交辞令。
2 裨谌（pí chén）：郑国大夫。
3 世叔：《左传》作"子太叔"（"太"、"世"二

At the time our Master made no reply, but when Nang gong Kuo had withdrawn he said, He is a true gentleman indeed, is that man! He has a right appraisal of 'virtue's power, has that man!

14.6

子曰："君子而不仁者有矣夫，未有小人而仁者也。"

【中译文】

孔子说："君子没有仁德的时候是有的呀，可是小人从来没有有仁德的时候。"

【英译文】

The Master (Confucius) said, It is possible to be a true gentleman and yet lack Goodness. But there has never yet existed a Good man who was not a gentleman.

14.7

子曰："爱之，能勿劳乎¹？忠焉，能勿诲乎？"

【中译文】

孔子说："爱他，能不让他勤奋吗？忠于他，能不教诲他吗？"

【注释】
1 �... 曰：「道之斯行」: 你如能提拔我; 而用
2 天下国家 (jiā): 泛指人人。
3 由、求：「由」指子路，「求」指《冉求》; 均用于

【译文】

冉有曰：「夫子为卫君乎?」子贡曰：
「诺, 吾将问之。」入曰：「伯夷、叔齐何人也?」

【英文】

The Master (Councilius) said, 'It is possible to be a true man and yet never was a good man who was not benevolent.'

goodness.

子曰：「......」

孔子说：「......」

孔子说：「君子之道三，我无能焉: 仁者不

【英文】

The Master (Councilius) said, How can he be said truly to love, who exacts no effort from the objects of his love? How can he be said truly to be loyal, who...

8.14

子曰：「不在其位，不谋其政。」

【译文】

【注释】
1 正: 纠正、端正。「正名」，端正名分。

【英文】

At the time Master out made no reply, but when Yang Kuo had gone
withdrawing... He is to be pitied... unwillingness... is indeed that the matter
has made...

bow's survey of that man.

9.14

【注释】

1 子西：春秋时，载入史籍的有三个子西。其一，楚国的公子申（楚平王的庶长子），曾任令尹（即宰相），有贤名，立楚昭王。他和孔子同时，死于孔子之后。其二，楚国的斗宜申。后谋乱被杀。生活在鲁僖公、鲁文公之世。其三，郑国的公孙夏，是子产（公孙侨）的同宗兄弟。曾掌握郑国政权，他死后，才由子产继他而执政。生当鲁襄公之世。本章的子西，或说指楚国的公子申，或说指郑国的公孙夏，已不可确考。

2 "彼哉"句：他呀，他呀。这是古代曾经流行的一个习惯用语，表示轻视，犹言算得了什么，不值得一提。

3 伯氏：名偃，齐国大夫。骈邑：齐国的地名。据清代阮元《积古斋钟鼎彝器款识》考证，今山东省临朐县柳山寨，即春秋时的骈邑，现仍残留有古城城基。

4 没（mò）齿：老到牙齿都掉没了。指老死，终身。无怨言：没有抱怨、怨恨的话。史载：伯氏有罪，管仲为宰相，奉齐桓公之命，依法下令剥夺了伯氏的采邑三百户。因管仲执法公允，所以伯氏口服心服，始终无怨言。

【英译文】

Someone asked about Zi Chan. The Master (Confucius) said, He was a

字古时通用），名游吉，郑国大夫。子产死后，继任郑国宰相。

4 行人：掌使之官（外交官员）。子羽：公孙挥，字子羽。郑国大夫。

5 东里：郑国邑名，在今河南郑州市，子产所居。子产：名侨，字子产。郑国大夫，后任宰相，有政声。

【英译文】

The Master (Confucius) said, When a ducal mandate was being prepared in the Zheng state Bi Cheng first made a rough draft, Shi Shu checked and revised it, Zi Yu the Receiver of Envoys amended and embellished it; Zi Chan of Dong Li gave it literary elegance.

14.9

或问子产，子曰："惠人也。"问子西[1]，曰："彼哉！彼哉[2]！"问管仲，曰："人也。夺伯氏骈邑三百[3]，饭疏食，没齿无怨言[4]。"

【中译文】

有人问到子产这人怎么样，孔子说："是宽厚大方的人。"问到子西，孔子说："他呀！他呀！"问到管仲，孔子说："是个人才。他剥夺了伯氏骈邑的三百户采地，伯氏只得吃粗粮，直到死也没有怨言。"

论语意解

【注释】

【英译文】

The Master (Confucius) said, When a ducal mandate was being prepared in the Zheng state Bi Cheng first made a rough draft, Shi Shu checked and revised it, Zi Yu the Receiver of Envoys amended and embellished it, Zi Chan of Dong Li gave it literary elegance.

14.9

或问子产。子曰："惠人也。"问子西。曰："彼哉！彼哉！"问管仲。曰："人也。夺伯氏骈邑三百，饭疏食，没齿无怨言。"

【中译文】

有人问郑国子产这个人怎么样，孔子说："是宽厚慈爱的人。"问到子西，孔子说："他呀！他呀！"问到管仲，孔子说："是个人才。他剥夺了伯氏骈邑的三百户，使伯氏只能吃粗粮，直到死也没有怨言。"

【英译文】

Someone asked about Zi Chan. The Master (Confucius) said, He was a kind-hearted man! Asked about Zi Xi he said, That man! That man! Asked about Guan Zhong he said, This is the sort of man he was: he could seize Pian with its three hundred villages from its owner, the head of the Bo Family; yet Bo, though he 'lived on coarse food' to the end of his days, never uttered a single word of resentment.

14.10

子曰:"贫而无怨难,富而无骄易。"

【中译文】

孔子说:"贫穷而没有怨恨,很难做到;富裕了而不骄傲,是容易做到的。"

【英译文】

The Master (Confucius) said, To be poor and not resent it is far harder than to be rich, but not presumptuous.

14.11

子曰:"孟公绰为赵、魏老则优¹,不可以为滕、薛大夫²。"

【英译文】

孔子说:"孟公绰做赵、魏两个大国的大臣,是非常称职的;但是却不可以做滕、薛这样的小国的大夫。"

论语意解

【注释】

1 孟公绰:鲁国大夫,属于孟孙氏家族。廉静寡欲而短于才。其德为孔子所敬重。老:古代对大夫家臣之长的尊称,也称"室老"。

2 滕,薛:古代两个小诸侯国。"滕",故城在今山东省滕州市西南十五里。"薛",故城在今山东省滕州市东南四十余里官桥至薛城一带。为何孟公绰不宜任小国的大夫呢?朱熹说:"大家势重,而无诸侯之事;家老望尊,而无官守之责。""滕、薛国小政繁,大夫位高责重。"所以,孔子说像孟公绰这种"廉静寡欲而短于才"的人,可以任大国上卿的家臣(望尊而职不杂,德高则能胜任),而不可以任小国的大夫(政烦责重,才短则难以胜任)。这说明了知人善任的重要性。

【英译文】

The Master (Confucius) said, Meng Gongchuo would have done well enough as Comptroller of the Zhao or Wei families; but he was not fit to be a State minister even in such a small state as Teng or Xue.

14.12

子路问成人¹。子曰:"若臧武仲之知²,公绰之不欲,卞庄子之勇³,冉求之艺,文之以礼乐,亦可以为成人矣。"曰:"今之成人者何必然?见利思义,见危授命,久要不忘平生之言⁴,

論語意解

14.10

子曰："贫而无怨难，富而无骄易。"

【中译文】

孔子说："贫穷而没有怨恨，难（做到）；富裕而不骄傲，是容易做到的。"

【英译文】

The Master (Confucius) said, 'To be poor and not resent it is far harder than to be rich, but not presumptuous.'

14.11

子曰："孟公绰为赵魏老则优，不可以为滕薛大夫。"

【中译文】

孔子说："孟公绰做赵、魏这两个大国的家臣，是很有余的；但是却不可以做滕、薛这样的小国的大夫。"

【英译文】

The Master (Confucius) said, 'Meng Gongchuo would have done well enough as Comptroller of the Zhao or Wei families, but he was not fit to be a State minister in such a small state as Teng or Xue.'

【注释】

1. 孟公绰：曾任鲁国大夫，属于高阳氏公族，廉静寡欲而迂。其需为不器皿轻重……者：古代诸侯大夫家臣之长。

2. 滕、薛：古代两个小诸侯国名。"滕"，故城在今山东省滕州市西南……"薛"，故城在今山东省滕州市南四十余里。

kind-hearted man! Asked about Zi Xi, he said, 'That man! That man!' Asked about Guan Zhong, he said, 'This is the sort of man he was: he could seize Pian Bo, with its three hundred villages from its owner, the head of the Bo family; yet Bo, though he lived on coarse food, to the end of his days, never uttered a single word of resentment.'

【英译文】

Zi Lu asked what a perfect man was. The Master said, "If anyone had the wisdom of Zang Wuzhong, the desirelessness of Meng Gongchuo, the courage of Bian Zhuangzi, the arts of Ran Qiu, and had graced these virtues by the cultivation of music and rites, then indeed I think we might call him a perfect man." Then the Master went on to say, "But why must the perfect man today be like that? In the face of profit let him think of justice. In the face of danger let him offer his life. In the face of long-standing poverty let him not forget his promise. Then he may be called a perfect man."

14.13

子问公叔文子于公明贾曰[1]："信乎，夫子不言、不笑、不取乎[2]？"公明贾对曰："以告者过也[3]。夫子时然后言，人不厌其言；乐然后笑，人不厌其笑；义然后取，人不厌其取。"子曰："其然，岂其然乎？"

【中译文】

孔子向公明贾问到公叔文子，说："是真的吗？他老人家不说、不笑、不取财。"公明贾回答说："这是传话的人言过其实了。他老先生是到适当的时候才说，别人就不讨厌他的讲话；快乐了然后笑，别人就不讨厌他的笑；符合礼义然后获取财物，别人就不讨厌他获取。"孔子说："是这样吗？真是这样吗？"

论语意解

三五六　三五五

亦可以为成人矣。"

【中译文】

子路问怎样才是一个完全意义上的人。孔子说："假若有臧武仲的明智，孟公绰的不贪，卞庄子的勇敢，冉求的多才多艺，再用礼乐以增文采，也就可以成为完全意义上的人了。"孔子又说："现在要成为完全意义上的人何必一定这样要求呢？只要他见到财利时能想到道义，遇到国家有危难而愿付出生命，长久处于穷困也不忘记平日的诺言，也就可以成为一个完全意义上的人了。"

【注释】

1 成人：完人；人格完备，德才兼备的人。

2 臧武仲：即臧孙纥（hé），臧文仲之孙。鲁国大夫，因不容于鲁国权臣而出逃。逃到齐国后，他预料到齐庄公不能长久，便设法拒绝了齐庄公给他的田，孔子认为他很明智（见《左传·襄公二十三年》）。

3 卞庄子：鲁国大夫，封地在卞邑（今山东省泗水县东）。传说他曾一个人去打虎，以勇著称。一说，即孟庄子。

4 久要：长久处于穷困的境遇。"要（yāo）"，通"约"。穷困。一说，"久要"即旧约，旧时答应过别人的话，从前同别人约定的事。平生：平日。

【英译文】

Zi Lu asked what a perfect man was. The Master said, "If anyone had the wisdom of Zang Wuzhong, the desirelessness of Meng Gongchuo, the courage of Bian Zhuangzi, the arts of Ran Qiu, and had graced these virtues by the cultivation of music and rites, then indeed I think we might call him a perfect man." Then the Master went on to say, "But why must the perfect man today be like that? In the face of profit let him think of justice. In the face of danger let him offer his life. In the face of long-standing poverty let him not forget his promise. Then he may be called a perfect man."

14.13

子问公叔文子于公明贾曰:"信乎,夫子不言,不笑,不取乎?"公明贾对曰:"以告者过也。夫子时然后言,人不厌其言;乐然后笑,人不厌其笑;义然后取,人不厌其取。"子曰:"其然?岂其然乎?"

【中译文】

孔子向公明贾问到公叔文子,说:"是真的吗?他老人家不言语,不笑,不取(财物)?"公明贾回答说:"这是传话的人说错了。他老先生是到该说话的时候才说话,别人就不讨厌他的话;快乐了然后才笑,别人不讨厌他笑;该取得的财物才取,别人也不讨厌他取。"孔子说:"是这样吗?真是这样吗?"

亦可以为成人矣。"

【中译文】

子路问怎样才是一个完全意义上的人。孔子说:"假若有臧武仲的明智,孟公绰的不贪,卞庄子的勇敢,再加上冉求的多才多艺,又能以礼乐来成就文采,也就可以成为完全意义上的人了。"孔子又说:"现在完全意义上的人何必一定要这样要求呢?只是看见利益时想到仁义,遇到国家有危难而能挺身出生命,长久处于困窘而不忘记平日的诺言,也就可以成为一个完全意义上的人了。"

【注释】

1 成人:完人,人格完善、德才兼备的人。
2 臧武仲:即臧孙纥(he),臧文仲之孙,曾国大夫,因不容于鲁国权臣而出走,逃到齐国后,他预料到季...出公不能长久,便拒绝法孙纥了齐庄公给他的田。孔子以为他明智(见《左传·襄公二十三年》)。
3 卞庄子:鲁国大夫,封地在卞邑(今山东省泗水县)。传说他曾一个人去打虎,以勇著称。一说,即卞严子。
4 久要:长久处于穷困的遭遇。"要"(yao)同"约","困","要","约",即旧约,旧的诺言。故旧即指从前同别人约定的事。平生:平日。

【注释】

1 公叔文子：名拔（一作发）。卫国大夫，卫献公之孙。死后谥"文"，故称公叔文子。公明贾：姓公明，名贾。卫国人。公叔文子的使臣。一说，"公明"即"公羊"，是《礼记》中说的公羊贾。

2 夫子：敬称公叔文子。

3 过：说得过分，传话传错了。

【英译文】

The Master (Confucius) asked Gongming Jia about Gongshu Wenzi saying, Is it a fact that your master neither 'spoke nor laughed nor took'? Gongming Jia replied saying, The people who told you this were exaggerating. My master never spoke till the time came to do so; with the result that people never felt that they had had too much of his talk. He never laughed unless he was delighted; so people never felt they had had too much of his laughter. He never took unless it was right to do so, so that people never felt he had done too much taking. The Master said, Was that so? Can that really have been so?

14.14

子曰："臧武仲以防求为后于鲁[1]，虽曰不要君[2]，吾不信也。"

【中译文】

孔子说："臧武仲凭借封地"防"而请求鲁国国君在鲁国立其后人为大夫，虽然有人说这样做不是要挟

君主，可我不相信。"

【注释】

1 "臧武"句："防"，鲁国地名，在今山东省费县东北六十里的华城，紧靠齐国边境，是臧武仲受封的地方。公元前550年（鲁襄公二十三年），臧武仲因帮助季氏废长立少得罪了孟孙氏，逃到邻近邾国。不久，他又回到他的故邑防城，向鲁国国君请求为臧氏立后代（让他的子孙袭受封地，并任鲁国大夫）。言辞甚逊。但言外之意：否则将据邑以叛。得到允许后，他逃亡到齐国（见《左传?襄公二十三年》）。

2 要（yāo）：胁迫，要挟。

【英译文】

The Master (Confucius) said, Zang Wuzhong occupied the fief of Fang and then demanded from the prince of Lu that (his brother) Wei should be allowed to take the fief over from him. It is said that he applied no pressure upon his prince; but I do not believe it.

14.15

子曰："晋文公谲而不正[1]，齐桓公正而不谲[2]。"

【中译文】

孔子说："晋文公狡诈不正派；齐桓公正派而不狡诈。"

论语意解

三五七

三五八

君主,但我不相信。"

【注释】

1. 臧武仲:即"臧孙纥",曾任鲁国大夫。防:是鲁国地名,在今山东省费县东北六十里防山附近。据鲁国旧城,是臧武仲的封地。公元前550年(鲁襄公二十三年),臧武仲因帮助季孙氏立少得罪于孟孙氏,遂逃奔邾国,又逃奔齐国。本人。他又回到他的故邑防城,向鲁国请求来为臧氏立后(由他的异母兄为臧氏之后),并在鲁国大夫面前表明不敢以此要挟君主之意。否则就据城以叛,得到允许后,他逃亡到齐国去了(见《左传·襄公二十三年》)。

2. 要(yāo):胁迫,要挟。

【英译文】

The Master (Confucius) said, Zang Wuzhong occupied the fief of Fang and then demanded from the prince of Lu that (his brother) Wei should be allowed to take the fief over from him. It is said that he applied no pressure upon his prince; but I do not believe it.

14.15

子曰:"晋文公谲而不正,齐桓公正而不谲。"

【中译文】

孔子说:"晋文公诡诈而不正派;齐桓公正派而不诡诈。"

【注释】

1. 公叔文子:名拔(一作发),卫献公之孙,故称公孙文子。卫国大夫,卫献公之孙。死后谥"文",故称公叔文子。公明贾:姓公明,名贾,卫国人。"公明"即《礼记》中所称之公明仪。

2. 夫子:此指公叔文子。

3. 时:说得其时,恰合时情况下。

【英译文】

The Master (Confucius) asked Gongming Jia about Gongshu Wenzi saying, Is it a fact that your master spoke neither, spoke nor laughed nor took? Gongming Jia replied saying, The people who told you this were exaggerating. My master never spoke till the time came to do so; with the result that people never felt that they had had too much of his talk. He never laughed unless he was delighted, so people never felt they had had too much of his laughter. He never took unless it was right to do so, so that people never felt he had done too much taking. The Master said, Was that so? Can that really have been so?

14.14

子曰:"臧武仲以防求为后于鲁,虽曰不要君,吾不信也。"

【中译文】

孔子说:"臧武仲借凭据引退,凭借国邑来要挟国君在鲁国立其后人之大夫,虽然有人说这样做不是要挟君主,但是我是不相信的。"

14.16

子路曰："桓公杀公子纠[1]，召忽死之[2]，管仲不死。"曰："未仁乎？"子曰："桓公九合诸侯[3]，不以兵车[4]，管仲之力也！如其仁！如其仁！"

【中译文】

子路说："齐桓公杀了公子纠，召忽自杀殉主，但管仲却没有自杀。"子路又说："这样，管仲算是没有仁德吧"孔子说："齐桓公多次召集各诸侯国，主持盟会，没用武力，而制止了战争，这都是管仲的功劳啊！这算得上是仁德！这算得上是仁德！"

【注释】

1 公子纠：小白（即后来的齐桓公）的哥哥。他二人都是齐襄公的弟弟。襄公无道，政局混乱，他二人怕受连累，于是，小白由鲍叔牙事奉逃亡莒国，公子纠由管仲、召忽事奉逃亡鲁国。而后，齐襄公被公孙无知杀死，公孙无知立为君。次年，雍廪又杀死公孙无知，齐国当时就没有国君了。在鲁庄公发兵护送公子纠要回齐国即位的时候，小白用计抢先回到齐国，立为君。接着兴兵伐鲁，逼迫鲁国杀死了公子纠（见《左传》庄公八年九年）。

2 召忽：他与管仲都是公子纠的家臣、师傅。公子纠被杀后，召忽自杀殉节。管仲却归服齐桓公，并由

论语意解

三六〇

三五九

【注释】

1 晋文公：春秋时有作为的政治家。晋献公之子，姓姬，名重耳。因献公宠骊姬，立幼子为嗣，他受到迫害，流亡国外十九年；后由秦国送回晋国，即位，为文公。他整顿内政，加强军队，使国力强盛。又平定周朝内乱，迎接周襄王复位，以"尊王"相号召。他伐卫致楚，"城濮之战"用阴谋而大败楚军。在践土（今河南省荥阳县 东北）大会诸侯，成为春秋时著名的霸主之一。公元前 636－前628年在位。谲（jué）：欺诈，玩弄权术，耍弄阴谋手段。

2 齐桓公：春秋时有作为的政治家。姓姜，名小白，姜尚（太公）的后人，齐襄公之弟。襄公被杀后他从莒 回国，取得政权。任用管仲为相，进行改革，富国强兵。 以"尊王攘夷"相号召，帮助燕国打败北戎，营救邢、 卫二国，制止戎狄入侵；又联合中原诸侯进攻蔡、楚， 与楚会盟于召陵（今河南省郾城东北）；还平定了东周 王室的内乱，多次与诸侯结盟，互不使用武力，使天下 太平了四十年。齐桓公成为春秋时第一个霸主。公元前 685－前643年在位。

【英译文】

The Master (Confucius) said, Duke Wen of Jin could rise to an emergency, but failed to carry out the plain dictates of ritual. Duke Huan of Qi carried out the dictates of ritual, but failed when it came to an emergency.

14.16

子曰：“晋文公谲而不正，齐桓公正而不谲。”

【译文】

孔子说：“晋文公诡诈而不正派，齐桓公正派而不诡诈。”

【注释】

1 晋文公：春秋时期著名的政治家、军事家。姓姬，名重耳。因献公受骊姬蛊惑，立奚齐为嗣，而受到迫害，流亡国外十九年。后由秦国资助回国夺位，即位后，地整顿内政，训练军队，使国力强盛，又平定周朝内乱，接捷周襄王复位，以"尊王"相号召，于城濮(今河南省范县、山东旧观城县一带)大会诸侯，故为春秋时期霸主之一。公元前636—前628年在位。谲(jué)：欺诈权术，变着圈套害事情。

2 齐桓公：春秋时代著名的政治家。姜姓，名小白。襄公(太公)的庶人。齐襄公之弟，襄公被杀后他自莒(qǔ)国，取得政权。任用管仲为相，进行改革，富国强兵。曾假"尊王攘夷"相号召，借机威慑诸侯，营救燕国，于召陵，制止北狄灭卫人侵；又联合诸侯使他及其中原；于葵丘会盟于封疆(今河南省睢县北)，以保天下王室的内乱。多次与诸侯结盟，可不便用武力，使天下大平了四十余年，齐桓公故为春秋时期第一个霸主。公元前685—前643年在位。

【英译文】

The Master (Confucius) said, Duke Wen of Jin could rise to an emergency but failed to carry out the plain dictates of ritual; Duke Huan of Qi carried out the dictates of ritual but failed when it came to an emergency.

益处。如果没有管仲，我们恐怕已经沦为披头散发、穿左开襟衣服的落后民族了。难道管仲该像一般的小百姓那样，为了守小节，在小山沟里上吊自杀，而不被人所知道吗？"

【注释】

1　一匡天下：使天下的一切得到匡正。"匡"，正，纠正。

2　微：非，无，没有。一般用于和既成事实相反的假设句前面。

3　被发左衽：当时边疆地区夷狄少数民族的风俗、打扮。"被"，同"披"。"衽（rén）"，衣襟。

4　匹夫匹妇：指一般的平民百姓，平庸的人。谅：信实，遵守信用。这里指拘泥小的信义、小的节操。

5　自经：自缢，上吊自杀。沟渎（dú）：古时，田间水道称沟，邑间水道称渎。这里指小山沟。

【英译文】

Zi Gong said, "I fear Guan Zhong was not benevolent. When Duke Huan slew his brother, he failed to follow his master in death. What is more, he became the slayer's Prime Minister." The Master said, "Through having Guan Zhong as his premier, Duke Huan became leader of the feudal princes and brought the world to a state of rectitude, so that to this very day the people are benefiting by what he then did for them. Without Guan Zhong, we might. Now wear our hair loose and fold our clothes to the left as the barbarians do. Must we expect from him what the ordinary men and women regard as true constancy to go off and strangle himself quietly at the side of a ditch?"

鲍叔牙推荐当了宰相。

3　九合诸侯：多次会合诸侯。"九"，不是确数，极言其多。一说，"九"便是"纠"，古字通用。"合"，集合。

4　不以：不用。兵车：战车。代指武力。

【英译文】

Zi Lu said, "When Duke Huan of Qi slew his brother Jiu, Zhao Hu (Jiu's teacher) followed him in death, but Guan Zhong (the other teacher of jiu) did not." Zi Lu went on saying, "Does this show that he fell short of virtue?" The Master said, "Many times Duke Huan convened the princes of all states without resorting to weapons or war-chariots; this is due to Guan Zhong. Such is his virtue! Such is his virtue indeed!"

14.17

　　子贡曰："管仲非仁者与？桓公杀公子纠，不能死，又相之。"子曰："管仲相桓公，霸诸侯，一匡天下[1]，民到于今受其赐。微管仲[2]，吾其被发左衽矣[3]。岂匹夫匹妇之为谅也[4]，自经于沟渎而莫之知也[5]！"

【中译文】

　　子贡说："管仲不是仁人吧？桓公杀了公子纠，管仲没自杀，却又辅佐桓公。"孔子说："管仲辅佐桓公在诸侯中称霸，匡正了天下，人民到如今还得到他的

【注释】

1. 一匡天下：使天下一切得到匡正。匡，正。

2. 微：非，无。名衽：……被迫不开明就成为野蛮民族了……

3. 被发左衽：当时边远地区某些少数民族的风俗，披发，"被"同"披"。"衽（rèn）"，衣襟。

4. 匹夫匹妇：指一般的平民百姓。平庸的人。谅：信实。

5. 自经：自缢，上吊。沟渎（dú）：田间水道和山沟。

【英译文】

Zi Gong said, "I fear Guan Zhong was not benevolent. When Duke Huan slew his brother, he failed to follow his master in death. What is more, he became the slayer's Prime Minister." The Master said, "Though having Guan Zhong as his premier, Duke Huan became the leader of the feudal princes and brought the world to a state of rectitude, so that to this very day the people are benefiting by what he then did for them. Without Guan Zhong, we might now wear our hair loose and fold our clothes to the left as the barbarians do. Must we expect from him what the ordinary men and women regard as true constancy to go off and strangle himself quietly at the side of a ditch?"

【英译文】

Zi Lu said, "When Duke Huan of Qi slew his brother Jiu, Zhao Hu (Jiu's teacher) followed him in death, but Guan Zhong (the other teacher of Jiu) did not." Zi Lu went on saying, "Does this show that he fell short of virtue?" The Master said, "Many times Duke Huan convened the princes of all states without resorting to weapons or war-chariots; this is due to Guan Zhong. Such is his virtue! Such is his virtue indeed!"

14.17

子贡曰："管仲非仁者与？桓公杀公子纠，不能死，又相之。"子曰："管仲相桓公，霸诸侯，一匡天下，民到于今受其赐。微管仲，吾其被发左衽矣。岂若匹夫匹妇之为谅也，自经于沟渎而莫之知也！"

【中译文】

子贡说："管仲不是仁人吧？桓公杀了公子纠，管仲不但没有自杀，却又辅佐桓公。"孔子说："管仲辅佐桓公，在诸侯中称霸，匡正了天下，人民到如今还受到他的好处……"

14.18

公叔文子之臣大夫僎与文子同升诸公[1]。子闻之，曰："可以为'文'矣[2]。"

【中译文】

公叔文子的家臣大夫僎，与文子一同在朝廷被升任为大夫。孔子听到这件事，说："公叔文子死后可以用'文'作谥号了。"

【注释】

1 僎（xún）：人名。原是公叔文子的家臣，由于文子的推荐，当上卫国的大夫。同升诸公：谓僎由家臣经公叔文子推荐而与之同为卫国的大夫。"公"，公室，朝廷。

2 为文：谥号为"文"。实际上，公叔文子死后，其子成请谥于君。卫君说：过去卫国遭荒年时，公叔文子曾煮粥赈济，施恩惠于饥民；又在国家危难时对君王表现非常忠贞。故给他的谥号是"贞惠文子"。

【英译文】

Gongshu Weizi, when summoned to office by the Duke of wei, brought with him and presented to the Duke his retainer Xun, the same Xun who became a State officer. The Master hearing of it said, With good reason was he accorded the title Wen.

14.19

子言卫灵公之无道也，康子曰："夫如是，奚而不丧[1]？"孔子曰："仲叔圉治宾客[2]，祝鮀治宗庙[3]，王孙贾治军旅。夫如是，奚其丧？"

【中译文】

孔子说到卫灵公的昏庸无道，季康子说："像这样为什么还不灭亡呢？"孔子说："有仲叔圉接待宾客办理外交，祝鮀主管祭祀，王孙贾统率军队。像这样的人协助政事，怎么会灭亡呢？"

【注释】

1 奚：为何，为什么。

2 仲叔圉（yǔ）：即孔文子。卫国大夫，世袭贵族。

3 祝鮀（tuó）：卫国大夫，世袭贵族。

【英译文】

The Master (Confucius) thought of Duke Ling of Wei as being no follower of the true Way. Ji Kangzi said, How is it then that he does not come to grief? The Master said, He has Zhong Shuyu to deal with foreign envoys and guests, the priest Zhu Tuo to regulate the ceremonies in his ancestral temple and Wang sun Jia to command his armies. Why then should he come to grief?

14.20

子曰："其言之不怍[1]，则为之也难。"

14.20

【译文】

The Master (Confucius) thought of Duke Ling of Wei as being un-followal of the true Way. It was Kang Zi said: How is it then that he does not come to grief?

The Master said: He had Zhong Shuyu to receive visitors and guests, the priest Tuo to maintain the ceremonies in the ancestral temple, and Wang Sun Jia to command the armies. With then should he come to grief?

14.19

【译文】

Gongshan Wei xi, when summoned to office by the Duke of Wei, wished him and his minister Xin, with him to the Duke his minister Xin, ... came a State officer. The Master treated it with good reason was he recorded the true Way.

过大夫，不敢不来报告。君主却说'去报告三位大夫吧！'"孔子到三位大夫那里去报告，他们表示不可以出兵。孔子说："因为我曾当过大夫，不敢不来报告。"

【注释】

1 陈成子：齐国大夫陈恒，又名田成子。他在齐国用大斗借粮、小斗收粮的方法，获得百姓拥护。政治上逐渐取得优势后，在公元前481年（鲁哀公十四年）杀死齐简公，掌握了齐国政权。此后的齐国在历史上也称"田齐"。简公：齐简公，姓姜，名壬。公元前484－前481年在位。

2 沐浴：洗头，洗澡。指上朝前表示尊敬与严肃而举行的斋戒。

3 告夫三子："三子"，指季孙氏、孟孙氏、叔孙氏。因当时的季孙、孟孙、叔孙权势很大，实际操纵鲁国政局，鲁哀公不敢作主，故叫孔子去报告这三位大夫。

4 从大夫之后：犹言我过去曾经当过大夫。参阅《先进篇第十一》第八章注。

5 之：去，往，到。

【英译文】

After Chen Chengzi assassinated Duke Jian of Qi, the Master bathed and went to court. He told Duke Ai of Lu, saying, "Chen Heng (i.e. Chen Chengzi) has murdered his prince. I petition that steps should be taken to

论语意解

三六六 三六五

【中译文】

孔子说："一个人大言不惭，那么他做起来也困难。"

【注释】

1 怍（zuò）：惭愧。这里是形容好说大话，虚夸，而不知惭愧的人。这种人善于吹嘘，自然就难以实现他所说的话。

【英译文】

The Master (Confucius) said, Those whose words are unrestrained will have difficulty in doing them all.

14. 21

陈成子弑简公[1]。孔子沐浴而朝[2]，告于哀公曰："陈恒弑其君，请讨之。"公曰："告夫三子[3]。"孔子曰："以吾从大夫之后[4]，不敢不告也。君曰'告夫三子'者！"之三子告[5]，不可。孔子曰："以吾从大夫之后，不敢不告也。"

【中译文】

陈成子杀了齐简公，孔子得知马上沐浴后上朝，向鲁哀公报告说："陈恒杀了君主，请出兵讨伐。"哀公说："去报告三位大夫吧！"孔子说："因为我曾经当

论语意释

【中译文】

孔子说："一个人大言不惭，那么他实践起来也困难。"

【注释】

1 怍（zuò）：惭愧。这里是形容吹牛的人，说多了，而不知所说的人。这种人善于吹嘘，自然做起来实现起来的时候。

【英译文】

The Master (Confucius) said, Those whose words are unrestrained will have difficulty in doing them all.

14.21

陈成子弑简公。孔子沐浴而朝，告于哀公曰："陈恒弑其君，请讨之。"公曰："告夫三子！"孔子曰："以吾从大夫之后，不敢不告也。君曰'告夫三子'者！"孔子曰："以吾从大夫之后，不敢不告也。"

【中译文】

陈成子杀了齐简公。孔子沐浴后去朝见鲁哀公，向鲁哀公报告说："陈恒杀了齐君，请出兵讨伐。"哀公说："去报告三位大夫吧！"孔子说："因为我曾经当

故大夫，不敢不报也。君曰'告夫三子'者。" 之三子告，不可。孔子曰："以吾从大夫之后，不敢不告也。"

【注释】

1 陈成子：齐国大夫田恒，又名田成子。他在齐国用大斗借粮的方法，小斗收粮的方法，来得百姓拥护，渐渐取得优势。在公元前481年（鲁哀公十四年）杀死齐简公，掌握了齐国政权，此后的齐国在历史上称"田齐"。简公：齐简公，名壬。公元前484－前481年在位。

2 沐浴：洗头、沐浴。指上朝前表示尊敬长辈而举行的斋戒。

3 告夫三子："三子"，指季孙氏、孟孙氏、叔孙氏，因当时的季孙、孟孙、叔孙权势很大，实际操纵鲁国政局，鲁哀公不敢作主，故明孔子去报告这三位大夫。

4 从大夫之后：谦言自己曾经当过这位大夫。参阅《先进篇第十一》第八章注。

5 之：去、往、到。

【英译文】

After Chen Chengzi assassinated Duke Jian of Qi, the Master bathed and went to court. He told Duke Ai of Lu, saying, "Chen Heng (i.e. Chen Chengzi) has murdered his prince. I petition that steps should be taken to punish him." The Duke said, "Tell it to the three lords (the heads of the three great families of Ji, Shu and Meng)!"

The Master (Confucius) said, "As I was once a lord, I was obliged to abide by the rites and tell my prince, and now your highness instructs me to tell the three lords."

The Master (Confucius) did so, and they did not approve his suggestion. The Master then repeated, "As I was once a lord, I was abliged to by rites and tell you."

14.22

子路问事君。子曰："勿欺也，而犯之[1]。"

【中译文】

子路问怎样事奉君主。孔子说："不要欺骗他，但可以当仁不让，有所冒犯。"

【注释】

1 犯：触犯，冒犯。这里引申为对君主犯颜诤谏。

【英译文】

Zi Lu asked how to serve the prince. The Master said, "Don't deceive him! But offer your exhortations if you have any objections."

14.23

子曰："君子上达，小人下达。"

【中译文】

孔子说："君子眼界与心胸向上通达；小人眼界与心胸向下拘泥。"

【英译文】

The Master (Confucius) said, The gentleman can influence those who are above him; the petty man can only influence those who are below him.

14.24

子曰："古之学者为己，今之学者为人。"

【中译文】

孔子说："古代求学的人，是为了充实提高自己；现在学习的人，是为了给别人炫耀。"

【英译文】

The Master (Confucius) said, In old days men studied for the sake of self-improvement; nowadays men study so as to impress other people.

14.25

蘧伯玉使人于孔子[1]，孔子与之坐而问焉，曰："夫子何为？"对曰："夫子欲寡其过而未能也。"使者出，子曰："使乎！使乎！"

论语意释

14.22

陈成子弑简公。孔子沐浴而朝，告于哀公曰："陈恒弑其君，请讨之。"公曰："告夫三子。"孔子曰："以吾从大夫之后，不敢不告也。君曰'告夫三子'者！"之三子告，不可。孔子曰："以吾从大夫之后，不敢不告也。"

【中译文】

陈成子杀了齐简公。孔子沐浴上朝，向鲁哀公报告说："陈恒杀了他的君主，请派兵讨伐他。"哀公说："你去向那三位大臣报告吧。"孔子（退下）说："因为我曾经做过大夫，不敢不来报告，君主却说'去向那三位大臣报告'呀！"孔子去向那三位大臣报告，三位大臣不同意（出兵讨伐）。孔子说："因为我曾经做过大夫，不敢不来报告呀。"

【英译文】

punish him." The Duke said, "Tell it to the three great families of Ji, Shu and Meng]!"
The Master (Confucius) said, "As I was once a lord, I was obliged to abide by the rites and tell my prince, and now your highness instructs me to tell the three lords."
The Master (Confucius) did so, and they did not approve his suggestion. The Master then repeated, "As I was once a lord, I was obliged to by rites and tell you."

14.23

子路问事君。子曰："勿欺也，而犯之。"

【中译文】

子路问怎样奉事君主。孔子说："不要欺瞒他，但可以当面不止，有所冒犯。"

【注释】

1 犯：触犯，冒犯。这里引申为对君主观点的争辩。

【英译文】

Zi Lu asked how to serve the prince. The Master said, "Don't deceive him! But offer your exhortations if you have any objections."

14.24

子曰："君子上达，小人下达。"

【中译文】

孔子说："君子服从义而向上通达；小人服从利向下通达。"

【英译文】

The Master (Confucius) said, The gentleman can influence those who are above him; the petty man can only influence those who are below him.

14.25

子曰："古之学者为己，今之学者为人。"

【中译文】

孔子说："古代求学的人，是为了充实提高自己；现在学习的人，是为了给别人炫耀。"

【英译文】

The Master (Confucius) said, In old days men studied for the sake of self-improvement; nowadays men study so as to impress other people.

【中译文】

蘧伯玉派使者去看望孔子，孔子让他坐下，问道："他老先生近来在做些什么？"使者回答说："他老先生想少犯些错误，却常常觉得没能做到。"使者走了以后，孔子说："好使者啊！好使者啊！"

【注释】

1 蘧（qú）伯玉：姓蘧，名瑗，字伯玉，卫国大夫。孔子去卫国时，曾住在他家里。当时，蘧伯玉是有名的有道德修养的人，古人对他颇多赞誉，如"蘧伯玉年五十而知四十九年非"（《淮南子·原道训》），"蘧伯玉行年六十而六十化"（《庄子·则阳篇》）。所谓化就是"与日俱新，随年变化"（郭庆藩《庄子集释》）之意。从本章所叙也可看出：使者说的话很谦卑，而由此却越能显出蘧伯玉善于改过的贤德。

【英译文】

Qu Boyu sent a messenger to the Master. The Master bade the man be seated and asked of him saying, What is your master doing? He replied, saying, My master is trying to diminish the number of his faults; but he has not been successful. After the messenger had left, the Master said, What a messenger, what a messenger!

14.26

子曰："不在其位，不谋其政¹。"曾子曰²："君子思不出其位³。"

【中译文】

孔子说："不在那个职位，就不要谋划那方面的政事。"曾子说："君子考虑事情，不超出他职责范围。"

【注释】

1 "不在"句：已见前《泰伯篇第八》第十四章，可参阅。
2 曾子：曾参。参阅《学而篇第一》第四章注。
3 "君子"句：本句也见于《周易·艮卦·象辞》："君子以思不出其位。"

【英译文】

The Master (Confucius) said, He who holds no rank in a State does not discuss its policies, Zeng Zi said, A true gentleman never thinks of anything beyond his duties.

14.27

子曰："君子耻其言而过其行。"

【中译文】

孔子说："君子以说得好而做得不好为耻辱。"

【英译文】

The Master (Confucius) said, A gentleman is ashamed to let his words outrun his deeds.

论语新解

14.26

子曰："不在其位，不谋其政。"曾子曰："君子思不出其位。"

【中译文】

孔子说："不在那个职位，就不要谋划那方面的政事。"曾子说："君子考虑事情，不超出他职责范围。"

【注释】

1. "不在"句：已见前《泰伯篇第八》第十四章，可参阅。
2. 曾子：参阅《学而篇第一》第四章注。
3. "君子"句：本句也见于《周易·艮卦·象辞》："君子以思不出其位。"

【英译文】

The Master (Confucius) said, He who holds no rank in a State does not discuss its policies. Zeng Zi said, A true gentleman never thinks of anything beyond his duties.

14.27

子曰："君子耻其言而过其行。"

【中译文】

孔子说："君子以说得多而做得不够为耻辱。"

【英译文】

The Master (Confucius) said, A gentleman is ashamed to let his words outrun his deeds.

14.28

蘧伯玉派使者去看望孔子，孔子让他坐下，问道："你的先生最近在做些什么？"使者回答说："他老先生想少犯些错误，却常常觉得没能做到。"使者走了以后，孔子说："好使者啊！好使者啊！"

【注释】

1. 蘧（qú）伯玉：姓蘧，名瑗，字伯玉，卫国大夫。孔子去卫国时，曾住在他家里。当时，蘧伯玉是有名的有贤德的人。古人对他赞誉极多，如："蘧伯玉年五十而知四十九年非。"（《淮南子·原道训》）,"蘧伯玉行年六十而六十化。"（《庄子·则阳篇》）所谓"化"就是"日日新，随年变化。"《韩其萧《庄子浅释》》之意。从本章叙述中可看出，他善于检讨反省自己，而且此种越能显出蘧伯玉善于反省的贤德。

【英译文】

Qu Boyu sent a messenger to the Master. The Master bade the man be seated and asked of him saying, What is your master doing? He replied, My master is trying to diminish the number of his faults, but he has not been successful. After the messenger had left, the Master said, What a messenger, what a messenger!

【注释】

1 方：同"谤"。指责，说别人的坏处。一说，比长较短。句中的意思则是：子贡喜欢将人拿来做比较，评论其短长。

2 不暇：没有空闲的时间。

【英译文】

Zi Gong was always criticizing other people. The Master said, It is fortunate for Ssu that he is so perfect himself as to have time to spare for this. I myself have none.

14.30

子曰："不患人之不己知[1]，患其不能也。"

【英译文】

孔子说："不忧虑别人不知道自己的学问与道德，只忧虑自己无能。"

【注释】

1 患：忧虑，担心，怕。

【英译文】

The Master (Confucius) said, A gentleman isn't concerned that people do not recognize his merits; he is concerned about his own incapacities.

论语意解

14.28

子曰："君子道者三，我无能焉：仁者不忧，知者不惑，勇者不惧。"子贡曰："夫子自道也！"

【中译文】

孔子说："君子之道有三条；我都没能做到：仁爱的人不忧愁，智慧的人不迷惑，勇敢的人不畏惧。"子贡说："这正是老师讲自己啊！"

【英译文】

The Master (Confucius) said, The Ways of the true gentleman are three. I myself have met with success in none of them. For he that is really Good is never unhappy, he that is really wise is never perplexed, he that is really brave is never afraid. Zi Gong said, The Master is your own Way!

14.29

子贡方人[1]。子曰："赐也贤乎哉？夫我则不暇[2]。"

【中译文】

子贡指摘别人。孔子说："赐呀，你就那么好吗？要叫我呀，可没有那种闲工夫。"

论语意释

14.28

子曰："君子道者三，我无能焉：仁者不忧，知者不惑，勇者不惧。"子贡曰："夫子自道也！"

【中译文】

孔子说："君子之道有三条，我都没有能够做到：仁德的人不忧愁，智慧的人不迷惑，勇敢的人不畏惧。"子贡说："这正是老师谦讲自己啊！"

【英译文】

The Master (Confucius) said, The Ways of the true gentleman are three. I myself have met with success in none of them. For he that is really Good is never unhappy, he that is really wise is never perplexed, he that is really brave is never afraid. Zi Gong said, The Master is your own Way!

14.29

子贡方人。子曰："赐也贤乎哉？夫我则不暇。"

【中译文】

子贡讥评别人。孔子说："赐呀，你就那么好吗？我可没有那种闲工夫。"

【注释】

1. 方："谤"，指别人的不是。一说，比。
卡较短。句中的意思应是：子贡喜欢执人拿来相比较，评论其短长。
2. 不暇：没有空闲的时间。

【英译文】

Zi Gong was always criticizing other people. The Master said, It is fortunate for Ssu that he is so perfect himself as to have time to spare for this; I myself have none.

14.30

子曰："不患人之不己知，患其不能也。"

【英译文】

孔子说："不忧虑别人不知道自己的学问志道德，只忧虑自己无能。"

【注释】

1. 患：忧虑，担心。怕。

【英译文】

The Master (Confucius) said, A gentleman isn't concerned that people do not recognize his merits; he is concerned about his own incapacities.

到处游说？岂不成了花言巧语的人吗？”孔子说：“我不敢花言巧语，而是恨那些固执的人。”

【注释】

1 微生亩：姓微生，名亩。传说是一位年长的隐士一作“尾生亩”。又说，即微生高。

2 栖栖（xī）：忙碌不安，到处奔波不安定的样子。

3 佞：花言巧语，能言善辩，卖弄口才。

【英译文】

Weisheng Mu said to the Master, "Why do you keep flitting from one place to another preaching? Is it not simply to show off the fact that you are a clever talker?" The Master said, "I have no desire to be thought a clever talker, but I do hate the stubbornness in those I try to convince."

14. 33

子曰：“骥不称其力¹，称其德也²。”

【中译文】

孔子说：“千里马，值得称赞的不是它的力气，而是它驯良的品性。”

【注释】

1 骥（jì）：古代称善跑的千里马。

2 德：这里指千里马能吃苦耐劳的优良品质。

论语意解

---

14. 31

子曰：“不逆诈¹，不亿不信²，抑亦先觉者，是贤乎！”

【中译文】

孔子说：“不事先怀疑别人欺诈，不主观猜测别人不诚信，但若遇上欺诈或不诚信的人却也能及早地发现察觉，这样的人该是贤人吧！。”

【注释】

1 逆：预先，预测。

2 亿：同“臆”。主观推测，猜测。

【英译文】

The Master (Confucius) said, Is it the man who 'does not count beforehand upon the falsity of others nor reckon upon promises not being kept', or he who is conscious beforehand of deceit, that is the true sage?

14. 32

微生亩谓孔子曰¹：“丘，何为是栖栖者与²无乃为佞乎³？”孔子曰：“非敢为佞也，疾固也。”

【中译文】

微生亩对孔子说：“孔丘，你为什么老是忙碌不安

14.31

子曰："不逆诈，不亿不信，抑亦先觉者，是贤乎！"

【中译文】

孔子说："不事先怀疑别人欺诈，不猜测别人不诚实，但若遇到主动上门来欺骗或不诚信的人，却能及早地察觉，这样的人就是贤人啊！"

【注释】

1 逆：预先。亿：同"臆"。

2 亿：同"臆"，主观揣测，猜测。

【英译文】

The Master (Confucius) said, Is it the man who 'does not count beforehand upon the falsity of others nor reckon upon promises not being kept', or he who is conscious beforehand of deceit, that is the true sage?

14.32

微生亩谓孔子曰："丘，何为是栖栖者与？无乃为佞乎？"孔子曰："非敢为佞也，疾固也。"

【中译文】

微生亩对孔子说……

【注释】

1 微生亩：姓微生，名亩。作"尾生亩"，义同。微生亩名高。

2 栖栖（xī）：忙碌不安，纷扰奔波不定的样子。

3 佞：花言巧语。能言善辩，卖弄口才。

【英译文】

Weisheng Mu said to the Master, "Why do you keep flitting from one place to another preaching? Is it not simply to show off the fact that you are a clever talker?" The Master said, "I have no desire to be thought a clever talker, but I do hate the stubbornness in those I try to convince."

14.33

子曰："骥不称其力，称其德也。"

【中译文】

孔子说："千里马，值得称赞的不是它的力气，而是称赞它自身的品德。"

【注释】

1 骥（jì）：古代称善跑的千里马。

2 德：这里指千里马能吃苦耐劳的好品质。

14.35

子曰："莫我知也夫[1]！"子贡曰："何为其莫知子也[2]？"子曰："不怨天，不尤人[3]，下学而上达。知我者其天乎！"

【中译文】

孔子说："没有人了解我啊！"子贡说："为什么会没有人了解您呢？"孔子说："我不埋怨天，也不归咎于人，下学人事，上达真理。了解我的大概只有天吧！"

【注释】

1 莫我知：即"莫知我"的倒装。没有人知道、了解我。

2 何为：为何。

3 尤：责怪，归咎，怨恨。

【英译文】

The Master (Confucius) said, The truth is, no one knows me! Zi Gong said, What is the reason that you are not known? The Master said, I do not 'accuse Hea ven, nor do I lay the blame on men'

But the studies of men here below are felt on high, and perhaps after all I am known; not here, but in Heaven!

论语意解

【英译文】

The Master (Confucius) said, "A steed is not praised for its strength, but for its fine qualities."

14.34

或曰："以德报怨何如[1]？"子曰："何以报德？以直报怨，以德报德。"

【中译文】

有人说："用恩德来报答仇怨，如何呢？"孔子说："那么用什么来报答恩德呢？应该以实事求是，公平无私来对待仇怨，用恩德来报答恩德。"

【注释】

1 以德报怨："德"，恩惠，恩德。"怨"，怨恨，仇怨。这话可能是当时的俗话。《老子》："大小多少，报怨以德。"这是老子哲学中一种调和化解矛盾的思想。孔子对这种思想提出了批评。

【英译文】

Someone said, What about the saying 'Meet resentment with kindness?' The Master said, In that case, how is one to meet kindness? Rather, meet resentment with upright dealing and meet kindness with kindness.

论语意释

14.35

子曰："莫我知也夫！"子贡曰："何为其莫知子也？"子曰："不怨天，不尤人，下学而上达。知我者其天乎！"

【中译文】

孔子说："没有人了解我啊！"子贡说："为什么说没有人了解您呢？"孔子说："不埋怨天，也不归罪于人，下学人事，上达真理。了解我的大概只有天吧！"

【注释】

1 莫我知：即"莫知我"，没有人知道。——了解。

2 何为：为何。

3 尤：责怪；归咎，怨恨。

【英译文】

The Master (Confucius) said, The truth is, no one knows me! Zi Gong said, What is the reason that you are not known? The Master said, I do not 'accuse Heaven, nor do I lay the blame on men.'

But the studies of men here below are felt on high, and perhaps after all I am known, not here, but in Heaven!

【英译文】

The Master (Confucius) said, "A steed is not praised for its strength, but for its inequalities."

14.34

或曰："以德报怨何如？"子曰："何以报德？以直报怨，以德报德。"

【中译文】

有人说："用恩德来报答怨恨，怎样呢？"孔子说："那么用什么来报答恩德呢？应该以公正来对待怨恨，用恩德来报答恩德。"

【注释】

1 以德报怨："德"，恩惠，恩德。"怨"，怨恨，仇怨。这句可能是当时的格言。《老子》:"大小多少，报怨以德。"这是道家哲学中一种调和折衷的思想。孔子对这种思想提出了批评。

【英译文】

Someone said, What about the saying 'Meet resentment with kindness'? The Master said, In that case, how is one to meet kindness? Rather, meet resentment with upright dealing and meet kindness with kindness.

【英译文】

Gongbo Liao spoke against Zi Lu to the Ji Sun. Zi Lu Jing Bo informed the Master saying. I fear my master's mind has been greatly unsettled by this. But in the case of Gongbo Liao, I believe my influence is still great enough to have his carcase exposed in the market-place. The Master said, If it is the will of Heaven that the Way shall prevail, then the Way will prevail. But if it is the will of Heaven that the Way should perish, then it must needs perish. What can Gongbo Liao do against Heaven's will?

14.37

子曰："贤者辟世[1]，其次辟地，其次辟色，其次辟言。"子曰："作者七人矣[2]。"

【中译文】

孔子说："贤人避开社会；其次是避开乱国；再其次是避开别人难看的脸色；再其次是避开难听的恶言。"孔子又说："这样做的已经有七人了。"

【注释】

1 辟世：指不干预世事而隐居。"辟"，同"避"。避开。

2 七人：指传说中的七位贤人隐士。具体所指其说不一。有的说是：伯夷，叔齐，虞仲（太公），夷逸，朱张，柳下惠，少连。有的说是：长沮，桀溺，荷蓧丈人，石门守门者，荷蒉者，仪封人，楚狂接舆。不可确考。

论语意解

14.36

公伯寮愬子路于季孙[1]。子服景伯以告[2]，曰："夫子固有惑志于公伯寮，吾力犹能肆诸市朝[3]。"子曰："道之将行也与，命也；道之将废也与，命也。公伯寮其如命何？"

【中译文】

公伯寮对季孙诽谤子路。子服景伯告知孔子，并说："季孙老先生已经被公伯寮迷惑住了，我的力量还能杀掉公伯寮把他的尸首摆到街市上去示众。"孔子说："道能得到实行，是天命；道被废掉，也是天命。公伯寮能把天命怎么样？"

【注释】

1 公伯寮：字子周。《史记·仲尼弟子列传》作"公伯僚"。一作"缭"。孔子的弟子。曾任季氏家臣。政治上的投机分子。愬（sù）：同"诉"。诬谤，告发，背后说人的坏话。

2 子服景伯：姓子服，名何，字伯，"景"是死后谥号鲁国大夫。

3 肆：指处以死刑后陈尸示众。市朝：被处死的罪犯中，自士以下的，陈尸于市集；自大夫以上的，陈尸于朝廷。

14.36

【英译文】

Gongbo Liao spoke against Zi Lu to the Ji Sun. Zi Lu-Jing Bo informed the Master, saying, I fear my master's mind has been greatly unsettled by this. But in the case of Gongbo Liao, I believe my great influence is still enough to have his carcass exposed in the market-place. The Master said, If it is the will of Heaven that the Way shall prevail, then the Way will prevail. But if it is the will of Heaven that the Way should perish, then it must needs perish. What can Gongbo Liao do against Heaven's will?

【原文】

公伯寮愬子路于季孙。子服景伯以告，曰："夫子固有惑志于公伯寮，吾力犹能肆诸市朝。"子曰："道之将行也与，命也；道之将废也与，命也。公伯寮其如命何？"

【中译文】

公伯寮向季孙毁谤子路。子服景伯告诉孔子，说："季孙先生已经被公伯寮的话迷惑了，我的力量还能够把公伯寮的尸首摆在市上示众。"孔子说："道能够得到实行，是天命；道得不到实行，也是天命。公伯寮能把天命怎么样？"

【注释】

1 公伯寮：字子周，《史记·仲尼弟子列传》作"公伯僚"。愬：一件"诉"，孔门弟子。孔子的学生，曾仕季氏家臣。肆诸市朝：陈尸示众。

2 子服景伯：鲁大夫，姓子服，名何，字伯，"景"是谥号，是孟献子曾孙。

3 肆：指陈尸示众。处死后陈尸示众，叫肆。古大夫以上，陈尸于朝；士以下，陈尸于市。

14.37

【原文】

子曰："贤者辟世，其次辟地，其次辟色，其次辟言。"子曰："作者七人矣。"

【中译文】

孔子说："贤人逃避动荡的社会而隐居，再次是逃避到另一个地方去，再其次是逃避别人难看的脸色，再其次是躲避别人难听的话。"孔子又说："这样做的已经有七人了。"

【注释】

1 辟世：避开乱世而隐居。辟，同"避"。

2 七人：指谁不可确指而且各说不一。具体所指其说不一。

Where are you from? Zi Lu said, From Master Kong. The man said, He's the one who 'knows it's no use, but keeps on doing it', is that not so?

14.39

子击磬于卫[1]，有荷蒉而过孔氏之门者[2]，曰："有心哉，击磬乎！"既而曰[3]："鄙哉，硁硁乎[4]！莫己知也[5]，斯己而已矣。'深则厉，浅则揭'[6]。"子曰："果哉！末之难矣。"

【中译文】

孔子在卫国，有一天正在敲着磬，有位挑着草筐从孔子门口经过的人，说："有心思啊，是敲磬吧！"过了一会儿，又说："鄙陋啊，那硁硁的声音，好像表明没有人了解自己，既然没有人了解，那就停止算了吧。这就好比过河'水深就穿着衣服过去；水浅就撩起衣服过去。'"孔子说："说得真果坚决啊！如果真像趟水那样，世上就没有什么困难了。"

【注释】

1 磬（qìng）：古代一种打击乐器，形状像曲尺，用玉或美石制成。

2 荷蒉："荷（hè）"，背，扛，担负。"蒉（kuì）"，草编的筐。《高士传》：荷蒉者，卫人也，避乱不仕，自匿姓名，故荷草器而自食其力也。

3 既而：不久，一会儿。

论语意解

三八〇 三七九

【英译文】

The Master (Confucius) said, Best of all, to withdraw from one's generation; next to withdraw to another land; next to leave because of a look; next best to leave because of a word. The Master said, The makers were seven.....

14.38

子路宿于石门[1]。晨门曰："奚自[2]？"子路曰："自孔氏。"曰："是知其不可而为之者与？"

【中译文】

子路在石门住宿。早晨看守城门的人问："你从什么地来？"子路说："从孔氏那儿。"守城门的人说："是那个知道难以做到而要坚持去做的人吗？"

【注释】

1 石门：鲁国都城（曲阜）外城的城门。一说，曲阜共有七个城门，南边的第二个门就叫石门。孔子第二次周游列国，道不能行，于六十八岁时，结束了他十四年的游说生活，率弟子们回鲁国的老家。子路打前站，先到石门，天已晚，在城门外住了一宿。

2 奚自："自奚"的倒装。从哪里来。

【英译文】

Zi Lu was spending the night at the Stone Gates. The gatekeeper asked,

【英译文】

The Master (Confucius) said, Best of all, to withdraw from one's generation; next to withdraw to another land; next to leave because of a look; next best to leave because of a word. The Master said, The makers were seven...

14.38

【中译文】

【注释】

【英译文】

Zi Lu was spending the night at the Stone Gates. The gatekeeper asked

Where are you from? Zi Lu said. From Master Kong. The man said, He's the one who knows it's no use, but keeps on doing it, is that not so?

14.39

【中译文】

【注释】

【中译文】

子张说："《尚书》上说：'殷高宗居丧守孝，三年不问政事。'为何这样呢？"孔子说："何止高宗这样，古人都这样。国君死了，文武百官都料理好自己的职事，听命于宰相三年之久。"

【注释】

1 "高宗"句：出自《尚书·无逸》篇。"高宗"，殷王武丁，为商代王朝第十一世的贤王。他即位后，用奴隶傅说（yuè）为相，又得贤臣甘盘辅佐，国家大治。武丁在位时，是殷王朝最隆盛的时代。"谅阴"，也写作"亮阴"，"谅暗"，"梁暗"。传统的读法是 liáng ān。其意历来学者说法各异：一、"亮"，同"谅"，诚信。"阴"，沉默。指武丁即王位之初，怀着满心的诚信，态度沉默，三年之中不大讲话。二、指武丁遭遇父丧，三年居丧守孝。后世帝王居守孝还沿称"谅阴"。三、指居丧时所住的房子。这种房子，只用一根梁作屋脊，周围没有楹柱，上边铺上茅草作檐，下垂于地。整个房子没有门窗，光线很暗。故称"梁暗"。此取第三说。"不言"，指不大过问政事。

2 薨（hōng）：周代诸侯之死叫"薨"。

3 冢（zhǒng）宰：商代官名，相当于后世的宰相。

【英译文】

Zi Zhang asked, "It is said in The Book of History, 'When King Gao Zhong

---

4 硁硁（kēng）：象声词。击石声。这里用来形容敲磬的声音。

5 莫己知也：好"莫知己也"。

6 "深则厉"句：出自《诗经·邶风·匏有苦叶》："匏有苦叶，济有深涉。深则厉，浅则揭。"大意是说大葫芦叶儿枯黄已经成熟，济水上有个看上去水挺大的渡口。如果水深，就穿着衣服下水过去；如果水浅，就撩起衣服趟过去。这里"荷蒉者"以涉水为喻，讥孔子不知己而不止，不能适浅深之宜。

【英译文】

The Master (Confucius) was playing the stone-chimes, when he was in Wei. A man carrying a basket passed the house where he and his disciples had established themselves. He said, How passionately he beats his chimes! When the tune was over, he said, How petty and small-minded! A man whose talents no one recognizes has but one course open to him-to mind his own business! 'If the water is deep, use the stepping-stones; if it is shallow, then hold up your skirts.' The Master said, That is indeed an easy way out!

14.40

子张曰："《书》云：'高宗谅阴，三年不言'。[1] 何谓也？"子曰："何必高宗，古之人皆然。君薨[2]，百官总己以听于冢宰三年[3]。"

论语意解

【英译文】

The Master (Confucius) was playing the stone-chimes when he was in Wei. A man carrying a basket passed the house where he and his disciples had established themselves. He said, How passionately he beats his chimes! When the tune was over, he said, How petty and small-minded! A man whose talents no one recognizes has but one course open to him—to mind his own business! If the water is deep, use the stepping-stones; if it is shallow, then hold up your skirts. The Master said, That is indeed an easy way out.

14.40

【英译文】

Zi Zhang asked, "It is said in The Book of History, When King Gao Zong of the Yin Dynasty was in mourning for his father, he did not speak about governing for three years.' What does this mean?" The Master said, "Not Gao Zong in particular. All men in the old days did so. Whenever a prince died, the successor went into mourning for three years, the ministers all continued in their offices, taking their orders from the Prime Minister."

14.41

子曰："上好礼则民易使也[1]。"

【中译文】

孔子说："在上位的人好礼，百姓就容易听从役使了。"

【注释】

1 使：使唤，役使。

【英译文】

The Master (Confucius) said, So long as the ruler loves ritual, the people will be easy to handle.

14.42

子路问君子。子曰："修己以敬。"曰："如斯而已乎？"曰："修己以安人[1]。"曰："如斯而已乎？"曰："修己以安百姓。修己以安百姓，尧舜其犹病诸[2]！"

【中译文】

子路问怎样才是君子。孔子说："修养自己，严肃恭敬的态度。"子路说："像这样就够了吗？"孔子说："修养自己，使别人安乐。"子路说："像这样就够了吗？"孔子说："修养自己，使全体百姓安乐。修养自己，使全体老百姓安乐，尧舜还不容易做到呢！"

【注释】

1 人：与"己"相对。这里当指士大夫以上的贵族、上层人士。比下面的"百姓"所指范围要窄。
2 病：担心，忧虑。

【英译文】

Zi Lu asked about the qualities of a true gentleman. The Master said, He cultivates in himself the capacity to be diligent in his tasks. Zi Lu said, Can he not go further than that? The Master said, He cultivates in himself the capacity to ease the lot of other people. Zi Lu said, Can he not go further than that? The Master said, He cultivates in himself the capacity to ease the lot of the whole populace. If he can do that, could even Yao or Shun find cause to criticize him?

14.43

原壤夷俟[1]。子曰："幼而不孙弟[2]，长而无述焉[3]，老而不死，是为贼[4]。"以杖叩其胫[5]。

【中译文】

原壤叉着两腿坐着等孔子。孔子说："你年幼时不

【英译文】

Yuan Rang sat waiting for the Master in a sprawling position. The Master said, Those who when young show no respect to their elders achieve nothing worth mentioning when they grow up. And merely to live on, getting older and older, is to be a useless pest. And he struck him across the shins with his stick.

14.44

阙党童子将命[1]。或问子曰:"益者与?"子曰:"吾见其居于位也[2],见其与先生并行也[3]。非求益者也,欲速成者也。"

【中译文】

阙党地方的一个童子来向孔子传信。有人问孔子:"他是要求上进的人吗?"孔子说:"我见他坐在大人的席位上,并与长辈并肩而行。他不是要求上进的人,而是一个想急于求成的人。"

【注释】

1 阙(què)党:鲁国地名,在今山东省曲阜市境内。一说,即"阙里",是孔子的家乡。将(jiāng)命:传达信息,传话。

2 居于位:坐在席位上。按古代礼节,大人可以有正式的席位就坐,儿童没有席位。可是,这位童子却与大人一起坐在席位上,可见其不知礼。

讲孝悌,长大了没有作为,老了还不死,简直是个害人的东西。"说着就用手杖敲了敲原壤的小腿。

【注释】

1 原壤:鲁国人,据说是周文王第十六子原伯的后人,是孔子多年的老朋友。《礼记·檀弓》记载:原壤的母亲死了,孔子去帮助他治丧,他却站在棺材上大声歌唱。孔子假装没听见,不去理会。跟从的人看不下去了,就劝孔子别帮原壤料理丧事了。孔子认为,无论如何,亲总是亲,故总是故,看在老朋友的份上,该帮他料理丧事,还要帮他料理。不过,孔子确也认为原壤是不礼不敬不近人情的。夷:指"箕踞",即屁股坐地,两条腿左右斜伸出去,叉开两只脚呈八字形。因像只簸箕故称。古人认为,以这种姿态坐在地上是一种轻慢无礼的表现。俟(sì):等待。

2 孙:同"逊"。弟:同"悌"。

3 长:长大,年长。无述:无作为,没成就,没贡献。

4 "老而"句:这句话孔子是专对原壤一人而发,有恨铁不成钢的意思。"贼",指为害社会的坏人。后世有人断章取义,把这句话连起来说成"老而不死是为"贼",误以为是孔子对老年人的一种侮骂。这显然与孔子本来的意思截然不同。

5 胫(jìng):小腿。

论语意解

论语意解

【英译文】

Yuan Rang sat waiting for the Master in a sprawling position. The Master said, Those who when young show no respect to their elders achieve nothing worth mentioning when they grow up. And merely to live on, getting older and older, is to be a useless pest. And he struck him across the shins with his stick.

14.44

原壤夷俟。子曰："幼而不孙弟，长而无述焉，老而不死，是为贼。"以杖叩其胫。

【中译文】

原壤叉开双腿一个童子来向孔子问信。有人问孔子："他是要来上学的人吗？"孔子说："我见他坐在有长者人的席位上，并且又拿着礼物而行。他不是要来上进的人，而是一个想急于求成的人。"

【注释】

1 原（que）壤：曾国地名，在今山东省曲阜市境内。一说："阙里"，是孔子的故乡。夷（jiāng）：蹲。俟：等待。

2 居于位：坐在席位上。据古代礼节，大人可以站正式的席位坐，儿童没有席位。可是，这位童子却占着大人一起坐在席位上，可见其不知礼。

3 长：长大。弟：无德。无述焉：毫无成就。贼：败坏。

4 "老而"句：这句话孔子是针对原壤一人而发。有些在不妨解的意思。"贼"，据孔书社来说此处不死是"贼"。因以为代表着如此人的一种轻蔑。这显然与孔子本来的意思略微不同。

5 胫（jìng）：小腿。

【中译文】

原壤叉开双腿坐着等待孔子。孔子说："幼年不讲孝悌，长了没有作为，老了还不死，简直是个害人的东西。"说着就用手杖敲了敲原壤的小腿。

【注释】

1 原壤：鲁国人。据说是周文王第十六子原伯的后人，是孔子少年时的老朋友，《礼记·檀弓》记载：原壤的母亲死了，孔子去帮助他治丧。他却敲着棺材上大声唱哥，孔子照做没听见，不走理会。别从的人看不下去了，就劝孔子别帮那种流氓理丧事，孔子说这是老朋友，故不忍弃。看在老朋友的份上，孔子也受够他了。不过，孔子简也以为他只是这课是不礼，本质还以人品的。果然，他"贤俟"，叉开腿坐在地上，又开着只脚竖立八字形。因此孔子，他说："古人叫这，这姿势变态坐在地上是一种对长辈无礼的表现。"

俟（sì）：等待。

2 孙："逊"。弟：同"悌"。

3 先生：这里是对年长者、长辈的尊称。

【英译文】

　　A boy from the village of Que used to come with messages. Someone asked about him, saying, Is he improving himself? The Master said, Judging by the way he sits in grown-up people's places and walks side by side with people older than himself, I should say he was bent upon getting on quickly rather than upon improving himself.

3. 夫子：这里是对孔子，长辈的尊称。

【英译文】

A boy from the village of Que used to come with messages. Someone asked about him, saying, Is he improving himself? The Master said, Judging by the way he sits in grown-up people's places and walks side by side with people older than himself, I should say he was bent upon getting on quickly rather than upon improving himself.

论语意译

Persevering yearly in to Learn odes and properly in the hall

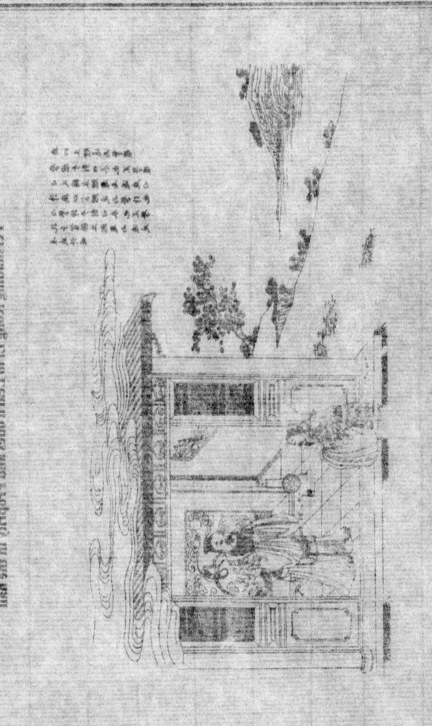

卫灵公篇第十五（共四十二章）

Confucius And His Students Talking about How to Gouern the State

15.1

　　卫灵公问陈于孔子[1]。孔子对曰："俎豆之事[2]，则尝闻之矣[3]；军旅之事，未之学也。"明日遂行[4]。

【中译文】

　　卫灵公向孔子询问如何列阵打仗。孔子回答说："礼节仪式方面的事，我曾听说；打仗方面的事，我没学过。"第二天就离开了卫国。

【注释】

1　陈：同"阵"。军队作战布列阵势。

2　俎豆之事：指礼节仪式方面的事。"俎（zǔ）"，古代祭祀宴享，用以盛放牲肉的器具。"豆"，古代盛食物的器具，似高脚盘。二者都是古代祭祀宴享用的礼器。

3　尝：曾经。

4　遂行：就走了。孔子主张礼治，反对使用武力。见卫灵公无道，而又有志于战伐，不能以仁义治天下，故而未答"军旅之事"，第二天就离开了卫国。

【英译文】

Duke Ling of Wei asked about the alignment of an army. The Master said, "I have learned some knowledge about rites; but I have never learned about military tactics." Then he left the next day.

15.2

　　在陈绝粮，从者病[1]，莫能兴[2]。子路愠见曰[3]："君子亦有穷乎？"子曰："君子固穷[4]，小人穷斯滥矣[5]。"

【中译文】

　　孔子在陈国断了粮，跟随的人饿坏了，不能站起身来。子路恼怒地对孔子说："君子也有困厄的时候吗？"孔子说："君子困厄时尚能安守，小人困厄了就胡作非为了。"

【注释】

1　病：苦，困。这里指饿极了，饿坏了。

2　兴：起来，起身。这里指行走。

3　愠（yùn）：恼怒，怨恨。

4　固：安守，固守。

5　滥：像水一样漫溢、泛滥。比喻人不能检点约束自己，什么事都干得出来。

论语意解

三九〇　三八九

卫灵公篇第十五 （共四十二章）

Confucius And His Students Talking about How to Govern the State

15.1

卫灵公问陈于孔子。孔子对曰："俎豆之事，则尝闻之矣；军旅之事，未之学也。"明日遂行。

【中译文】

卫灵公向孔子询问有关排兵布阵的事情。孔子回答说："礼仪方面的事情，我曾听说过；排兵布阵的事情，我没有学过。"第二天就离开了卫国。

【注释】

1 陈：同"阵"，军队作战布列阵势。

2 俎豆之事：指礼仪方面的事。"俎（zǔ）"、"豆"，古代祭祀和宴享用以盛放食物的器具，二者都是古代祭祀和宴享用的礼器。

3 军：军旅。

4 遂行：离去了。孔子主张礼治，反对使用武力。卫灵公无道，而又好志于战伐，不能以礼义安天下，故而未答"军旅之事"，第二天就离开了卫国。

【英译文】

Duke Ling of Wei asked about the alignment of an army. The Master said, "I have learned some knowledge about rites; but I have never learned about military tactics." Then he left the next day.

15.2

在陈绝粮，从者病，莫能兴。子路愠见曰："君子亦有穷乎？"子曰："君子固穷，小人穷斯滥矣。"

【中译文】

孔子在陈蔡断了粮，跟随的人病倒了，不能起来。子路愤怒地来见孔子说："君子也有困厄的时候吗？"孔子说："君子固守困厄而能镇定安守，小人困厄了就胡作非为了。"

【注释】

1 病：困。这里指饿倒下了，倒下了。

2 兴：起来，起身。这里指站起来。

3 愠（yùn）：恼怒，怨恨。

4 固：固守。

5 滥：像水一样漫溢，泛滥。由他人不能控制约束自己，什么事都干得出来。